"INDIANS! ON THE OTHER SIDE. ON HORSES!"

They had just gained the bank near the willow when the man who was in the lead saw them. He kicked the pinto, raising his rifle, just as Otio lifted the Spencer and drilled him through the neck.

"He is dead," Otio said walking up to the other one, a woman.

Suddenly she had drawn a knife and charged him. But he was quicker, stepping to the side and tripping her, while with the heel of his hand he smashed her in the lower back. She lay on the ground, doubled in pain, her breath coming in grunts. All at once, the fallen Indian woman uncoiled and dove at his legs. Seizing her arm, he swung it around behind her back. A cry broke as he pushed her down on her face and, after a moment, she stopped struggling.

Slowly Otio lessened the pressure on her arm and quickly turned her over on her back. She was not a woman at all. She was a young girl. A beautiful young girl . . .

EASY COMPANY

EASY COMPANY

AND THE SHEEP RANCHERS

JOHN WESLEY HOWARD

A JOVE BOOK

EASY COMPANY AND THE SHEEP RANCHERS

A Jove Book / published by arrangement with
the author

PRINTING HISTORY
Jove edition / October 1982

ISBN: 0-515-06353-3

Jove books are published by Jove Publications, Inc.,
200 Madison Avenue, New York, N. Y. 10016. The words
"A JOVE BOOK" and the "J" with sunburst are trademarks
belonging to Jove Publications, Inc.

PRINTED IN THE UNITED STATES OF AMERICA

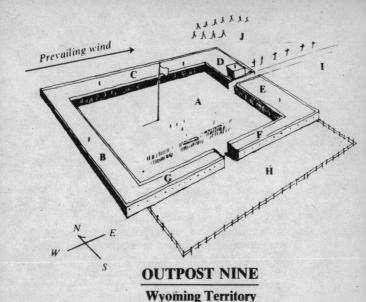

OUTPOST NINE

Wyoming Territory

KEY

A. Parade and flagstaff

B. Officers' quarters ("officers' country")

C. Enlisted men's quarters: barracks, day room, and mess

D. Kitchen, quartermaster supplies, ordnance shop, guardhouse

E. Suttler's store and other shops, tack room, and smithy

F. Stables

G. Quarters for dependents and guests; communal kitchen

H. Paddock

I. Road and telegraph line to regimental headquarters

J. Indian camp occupied by transient "friendlies"

INTERIOR   OUTSIDE

OUTPOST NUMBER NINE
(DETAIL)

Outpost Number Nine is a typical High Plains military outpost of the days following the Battle of the Little Big Horn, and is the home of Easy Company. It is not a "fort"; an official fort is the headquarters of a regiment. However, it resembles a fort in its construction.

The birdseye view shows the general layout and orientation of Outpost Number Nine; features are explained in the Key.

The detail shows a cross-section through the outpost's double walls, which ingeniously combine the functions of fortification and shelter.

The walls are constructed of sod, dug from the prairie on which Outpost Number Nine stands, and are sturdy enough to withstand an assault by anything less than artillery. The roof is of log beams covered by planking, tarpaper, and a top layer of sod. It also provides a parapet from which the outpost's defenders can fire down on an attacking force.

one ────────────

The tall, weathered Texan stood hard in front of Captain Warner Conway's desk, glaring at the commanding officer of Outpost Number Nine.

"Goddammit, Conway, I already know the army's gonna do all it can. That's what you soldiers always say. And what I'm saying is, what the hell good is that? I want you to do *more* than all you can!"

Warner Conway continued to look impassively at the redfaced, gravelly-voiced man standing before him, while out of the side of his eye he also took in First Lieutenant Matt Kincaid, standing across the room, and Elihu Cohoes's foreman, Ching Domino, who thus far had remained silent.

"I want protection for my herd, Conway, and I have got every right to expect that! Those thievin' red sons of bitches butchered one of my prime steers, goddammit!"

"Maybe you're lucky that's all they did," Conway said coolly, looking down at the back of his hand, and then bringing his eyes up to the cattleman's, "since you were trespassing on tribal land to begin with."

"What the hell do you mean!"

Conway got to his feet swiftly and crossed to the large wall map directly behind his two visitors. "Here." He pointed with his index finger. "Here's Horsehead Creek where you're holding your herd now. That right?"

Cohoes reached into the pocket of his faded hickory shirt and took out a wooden match and put it between his lips. "Right." He nodded, clipping off the word tightly, and began to chew on the match.

"And here"—Conway tapped a second area on the map with his middle finger—"here is where you say the Sioux killed your steer. Is that correct?"

Cohoes took a deep breath, his long nostrils flaring slightly. "That's the size of it. What the hell you gettin' at? They killed a steer, that's right."

Conway had turned back from the map and was facing the Texan squarely. Jerking his thumb over his shoulder, he said, "Horsehead Creek, where your herd is now, is on federal land."

"I know that!"

"But where your steer was killed—"

"And butchered, goddammit!" interrupted Cohoes.

"—is on tribal land," continued Conway, as though the cattleman had not spoken. "As I said, you were trespassing on tribal land."

"That is the goddamnedest bullshit I ever heard! What the hell kind of army are you, anyways?" Cohoes's fiery face whipped around to seek support from Ching Domino, but the foreman remained silent, a sneer curling his lip, his heavy eyes hooded as he stood loose, with his thumbs hooked into his heavy gunbelt.

Captain Warner Conway stood just as tall as the Texan. A man in his middle forties, distinguished, with graying hair at his temples, he was almost as lean and vigorous-looking as his adjutant and second-in-command, Matt Kincaid.

It was Kincaid who answered Cohoes now.

"We are here to protect everyone, Mr. Cohoes," he said as Conway walked back to the swivel chair behind his desk and sat down. "But the United States Army does not play favorites. We favor the law. Easy Company will do all that's necessary to protect your herd of cattle, but you must keep your beeves on federal land."

Ignoring Kincaid, Cohoes glared at Conway. "I am

2

saying one thing to you, Conway, and it is this. If I, by Jesus, see or even smell one of them red sons of bitches near my beeves, I will wipe that whole fucking tribe off of the face of God's green earth. So help me!"

Elihu Cohoes, known as a man not to be argued with, known all over the Panhandle as a man who didn't give a good goddamn about anyone, stood there chewing on the wooden lucifer, switching it from one side of his mouth to the other, with his eyes hard on Easy Company's CO. Now, hearing Kincaid move behind him, he canted his head at the lieutenant.

"Captain Conway and I have both heard you, mister," Matt said, and his words were not warm. "And the captain has given you his reply."

Cohoes glanced again at his foreman. Ching Domino was a man of average height with tight, olive-colored skin, closely spaced eyes, and, under his dirty black Stetson hat, shiny black hair. His clothes were tight on his body, looking, Matt thought, as though they'd been painted on him. He sure didn't look like a cattleman, and Kincaid wondered what he was really doing with a man like Cohoes, who was all steer and leather and no question about his way of life.

Cohoes, seeing that his foreman was still not going to speak, and indeed realizing it wasn't necessary, turned back to Conway, who was regarding him quietly.

Elihu Cohoes, a man of fifty-odd years, with a trail-hardened, leathery face and hands to match, looked as though that leather went all the way through. His nose was long, and he had the habit of rubbing it with his callused thumb—the way a horse will rub its nose along its extended foreleg, Conway thought as he watched now.

Blind in one eye, Cohoes generally turned his head slightly sideways when he spoke to someone. The mishap had occurred in a Fort Worth gambling establishment

3

when some frisky cow waddy had fired through one of the upstairs windows while racing his horse up and down that area known as the Cabbage Patch. It was pure chance that the bullet had streaked along the room occupant's cheek and across his eye. Though Cohoes had lost half of his sight, he had never lost his anger. It took a while for Cohoes to find the miscreant, but when he did, the fellow took up permanent residence in Fort Worth—or, rather, under it.

Ching Domino was remembering it, as a matter of fact, as he watched Cohoes rub his nose, for the story was well known; and now in Conway's office he began to ponder on how these damn fool soldier boys didn't know who they were by-God dealing with.

Conway had placed the palms of his hands flat on his desk, and now, leaning forward a little, he looked at Elihu Cohoes dead-center. "Mr. Cohoes..." he began, and Matt Kincaid noted the patience purring in the captain's voice. "Mr. Cohoes, I can only assure you for the last time that the army offers you full cooperation, to the extent of men and equipment available. Let me remind you once again that we are a single company of mounted infantry here at Outpost Number Nine, with an area to patrol that runs from the Bighorns to the South Pass; that includes the Absarokas and the High Plains. That is a whole lot of Wyoming, mister. And we are not only talking about a sizable territory, we are talking about the Sioux, the Cheyenne, and the Arapaho, not to mention a growing population of white settlers—all of whom want something from us."

"Our scalps, more often than not," Kincaid said. "I think Captain Conway is telling you that Easy Company will do all it can to protect your herd, but don't expect miracles." Kincaid had difficulty in not releasing a long sigh as he finished repeating simply what had been said at the very beginning.

Still, the Texan's hard face darkened. "Captain, I am telling it to you and the lieutenant once more; I got two thousand head of prime longhorns out there at Horsehead, which I aim to fatten up on Greybull grass 'fore pushing 'em up to the Stinking Water for seed stock and for shipping." He shifted his good eye over to Matt and then swung his gaze back to Conway.

"By God, I know men in Washington. You are not dealing with some half-assed sodbuster, sheep-dipper, or Injun lover. You are talkin', by God, to a Texas cattleman, and I want more than them maybes and all that shit. I want an escort and full army cooperation when I trail up to the Stinking Water, *and* I want you to do something about them red bastards what killed and butchered that longhorn, and for which I am billin' the army!"

Kincaid watched Conway's ears turn red, a sure sign of displeasure; but the captain's voice was as hard and even as a milled board.

"And Mr. Cohoes, I am telling you I will be listening to the other side on that matter—the Sioux. You will have your escort—provided I have men to spare—at the time you're ready to push up to the Stinking Water River."

The Texan, still exasperated, took his Stetson hat off his head and immediately put it back on again.

"What you figger, Ching?"

"That is a piss-poor effort at helpin' honest white men." It was the first he had spoken, and the words came out slow and heavy.

"My feelin's exactly," Cohoes said, with a hard nod of his head.

It seemed to Matt Kincaid that Conway's Virginia accent was more apparent when he spoke now; he knew this to be the case whenever the captain was really controlling his anger. "I will give you one other assurance, Mr. Cohoes. The United States Army in the Wyoming

5

Territory is, and will be, impartial. We do not take sides; we see that the treaties with the Indians are honored, and we strive to maintain law and order, keeping the peace where it is at all possible. This means, sir, that you and your men will also obey the law. Just remember this— if there is any fighting with Indians to be done around here, it will be the army that does it. I trust that this is quite clear!" Captain Conway stood, the knuckles of his two hands just touching the top of his desk.

"Captain Conway, I will be expectin' action on this, you better believe it." And with a snort, with a nod toward Ching Domino, and with that lucifer still in his teeth, Elihu Cohoes tromped out of the office, his foreman following with the very same sneer on his face that had been there when he entered.

When the door had closed behind them, Conway released a long sigh and reached for his box of cigars.

"Well, sir, they still breed 'em tough down in the Panhandle," Matt said with a wry grin.

The captain bit off the end of his cigar. "And cantankerous," he added.

They were silent a moment.

"So what do you think, Matt?"

Kincaid moved to the chair indicated by the captain and sat down. "Two things, sir. First, a visit to the Brulés, to see what Little Hawk has to say about that steer."

Conway nodded, lighting his cigar. Waving out the match, he said, "And second—Horsehead Creek?"

"Yes, sir."

"You'll take a squad?"

"A squad, and Windy if he gets back."

"Where is that lecherous old rascal?" asked Conway, his good humor returning with a rush.

Matt grinned. "Not at Tipi Town, for a change. He

6

is out scouting the prospects of game, and exercising his Delawares. He likes to keep those scouts sharp."

"Damned lucky for us he does." Conway released a cloud of smoke and, leaning back in his swivel chair, raised his eyes as the smoke floated toward the ceiling. "I am thinking about Ching Domino," he said suddenly.

"Funny thing, sir, so was I."

"I'll wager our thoughts were the same," Conway said, dropping his head down and looking directly at his second-in-command.

"If that boy is a cattle foreman..." Kincaid let it hang, opening his hands and shrugging.

"...then I'm a full-blooded Sioux," Conway finished.

"I almost dropped when he finally said something. Captain, he is one mean-looking son of a bitch."

"You are talking about his face, his body, and especially that tied-down Navy Colt that looks to have had plenty of use."

"I don't believe Ching Domino knows a cow from a jackrabbit, but I'll bet my last dollar he can shoot the eye out of a striking snake."

"Interesting, Cohoes wasn't carrying any hardware."

"A lot of cattlemen don't, sir."

Conway nodded. "I guess you don't need to, if you can afford to hire somebody to carry it for you, and Cohoes can sure do that."

Matt turned suddenly toward the window, listening. "It could be Windy, sir; he's due."

"Better have a look, then."

Matt Kincaid stood up. In his thirties, he was tall, but not stringy like Cohoes. He was tall and broad-shouldered, and at the same time lithe, narrow at the hips, and ruggedly handsome. Conway looked admiringly at his adjutant. Kincaid, serving his second tour of frontier

7

duty, was the man Warner Conway depended upon more than any other. Like Conway, Kincaid had been passed by for promotion, and like the captain, he seldom mentioned the fact. Conway knew that without Matt Kincaid, Outpost Number Nine would be a whole lot poorer.

Now, as Matt opened the door of the orderly room, they both heard the sentry calling from the lookout tower.

Private Billy Golightly, walking guard along the perimeter fence, had watched the red dawn spreading across the sky, turning to gold as it touched the east wall of Outpost Number Nine, and washing over Tipi Town, the little village of transient Indians that lay several hundred yards to the northeast. A jay called in the thin, chill morning air, and in the Indian village a dog began barking.

Billy Golightly, a raw recruit—no one seemed to know from where—was half dreaming of coffee and the pleasures of prone relaxation in his bunk when he was suddenly pulled right into the present as he heard hooves drumming toward the outpost. At that same moment, the picket guard called out.

"Two riders coming in! Windy Mandalian and a Delaware!"

Private Golightly had been well trained by his platoon sergeant, Gus Olsen, and by First Sergeant Ben Cohen. Quickly he brought his Springfield to port arms and headed for a stack of firewood that would afford him protection, should the report be a false one. Cohen and just about everyone else on the post had warned him how clever the hostiles were at calling out fake sentry reports or, during a skirmish, blowing false calls on a bugle, and sometimes even dressing up in soldiers' uniforms, causing enormous confusion.

In a moment two riders broke into view, and Private

Golightly was relieved to see that the picket guard's call had been true.

They were cantering in pretty fast; one on a blue roan, the other riding an Indian paint. The Delaware was sitting straight up on his pony's blanket-clad back, his muscular legs gripping the animal's flanks, his hands wrapped into its thick mane; his companion, on the roan, was dressed in fringed buckskin, and sat easy in a battered stock saddle. There was no mistaking them. It could only be Easy Company's chief scout and one of his men.

The big gates were opened from the inside, and the riders trotted briskly in. Henry Walks Quickly, the young Delaware, jumped off his pony, while Windy Mandalian, although seeming to move in a more leisurely manner, was actually on the ground at the same time.

At just that moment, Matt Kincaid came out of the orderly room and strode across the parade toward the gate.

Henry Walks Quickly, the Delaware, looked impassively at the officer, waiting. Windy sniffed, and then ejected a stream of tobacco juice at a pile of fresh horse manure on the parade.

"You're still in one piece," Matt said as he looked at the long, lean scout and his companion.

"Still got our hair." Windy's grin was sour. "And the Sioux still got theirs."

Matt turned to the Delaware. "You took good care of him, eh, Henry?"

The Delaware nodded. "We take good care," he said. "Now we want coffee."

"Go see Dutch in the mess hall." Then, when one of the stable detail had taken the horses, Matt turned back to Windy. "We'll go see the captain." And on the way across the parade he filled the scout in on the meeting with Elihu Cohoes and his foreman.

9

Conway waved Kincaid to a chair, while Windy took up his customary position next to the window, declining a formal seat.

"Could stand a cup of the Dutchman's jawbreaker," the scout said.

"It's on the way." Conway leaned forward on his desk, a cigar between the thumb and first finger of his right hand. There was a question in his eyes, but he knew there was no way you could hurry words out of Windy Mandalian.

Fortunately, at that moment there was a knock at the door, and it was Corporal Bradshaw, the company clerk, with coffee for the three of them.

"That is what I call service," Windy said with a grin.

Conway, studying him a moment, wondered whether he would take the plug of tobacco out of his mouth before drinking his coffee. He was relieved to see his chief scout lean forward and spit an enormous glob of tobacco and thick saliva into the cuspidor by his desk, right on target. The rank odor of chewed cut-plug wafted across the captain's desk, and he reached for his cigar.

Windy sighed, addressing his cup of coffee. Standing by the window, his hawk nose, sharp jaw, and piercing eyes were emphasized by the morning light that shone through it. Mostly, the sunlight accentuated his amazing likeness to an Indian. There were some who knew him, however—especially among the Sioux, the Cheyenne, and the Arapaho—who claimed he was at least one-quarter coyote and one-quarter grizzly.

Matt told Conway, "I briefed Windy on our meeting with Cohoes."

"Don't need no filling in," the scout said. "I know that type like the back of my hand. Coyote piss and buffalo shit from the feet up." He took a gurgling pull at his coffee. "Not bad for gunpowder coffee," he said.

"Got a bit of news. First, I seen them two riding off when I was coming in with Henry. The tall one, he is a cowman for sure, but the other, he sits that hoss like he had a spike up his ass. I'm talking about the one with the tied-down pistol, and the Winchester in his saddle boot. He is no good, that feller."

"We know that," Conway said. "Matt and I can't figure what he's doing punching cows."

"I reckon he ain't punched a single cow worth mention. He's a regulator. Now the question is, gents, what does this feller Cohoes want with a gunhawk?" And he dropped one eyelid while keeping the other wide open. A grin began to spread across his face, raising his whiskers along the sides of his jaw. They sat for a moment in silence, each with his coffee and his own thoughts regarding Cohoes and Ching Domino and the Texas cattle. Now both officers watched as Windy Mandalian, having finished his coffee, took out his plug of tobacco and sliced off a sizable chew with his Bowie knife. The two men, familiar with his ways, waited patiently, for it was clear he had more to say; as usual he was saving the best for last.

The scout's movements as he prepared his chew were deliberate—slow, sure, with nothing unnecessary to the accomplishment of his task. Both Conway and Kincaid knew that Windy could move with extraordinary speed when necessary, as any number of dead Indians might have testified.

The scout finally had his fresh chew working, moving it around in his jaws to work up flavor and consistency.

Conway had been watching him in fascination, as he often did, and now he said, "Well, if we can keep the Texans off Indian land, and the Brulés off those fat cattle, we might avoid trouble. Matt's going to pay Little Hawk a visit. Maybe you'd like to go along, Windy."

11

The scout nodded. "Like to see that old boy again. Me and him is old buddies."

Conway was studying Mandalian closely, unable to understand how he could hold such an enormous chunk of tobacco in his mouth and speak halfway intelligibly at the same time. Windy looked as though he had an apple in his cheek.

The scout leaned forward all at once, with no warning, and let fly at the captain's cuspidor. He missed.

"Shit. Well, mebbe I'm out of practice." He stretched, then settled into his easy self again. "'Pears to me, Captain Conway, we do have trouble coming up."

"You mean that steer?" Matt asked.

"I do not. I mean somethin' else."

"Something else?" Conway said. "What else? Will you please tell us, for Christ's sake?"

Windy shifted his chew to the other side of his mouth and looked again at the cuspidor, while Conway glared at him with impatience. But the scout was not perturbed. He spat with fair accuracy this time, and seemed pleased with himself, wiping his beard and sniffing.

Then he said one word. "Sheep."

"Sheep?" Conway echoed.

Windy nodded. "What every cattleman loves."

"Sheep, here?" Conway could hardly believe what he was hearing. "But this isn't sheep country!"

"It might be about to be, Captain. There is a flock of about fifteen hundred woollies on its way down from the Absarokas. Should be around here in a day or two."

"You mean they are actually headed for Number Nine?" Kincaid asked.

"Told 'em they better, if they want to find out how to keep their hair in this here country." And Windy lowered both eyelids this time, then opened them real wide. "You know what'll happen if the Brulé get wind of 'em.

12

And I expect they know about them by now."

"And when Cohoes and his bunch meet those sheep," said Conway, "it'll not be any social event." And he shook his head.

"Those cattlemen and sheepmen might make the Indians seem kinda tame," Windy observed. "'Specially when I tell you what sort of gentleman is ramrodding them woollies."

Conway and Kincaid both stared at him in surprise. "You mean," said Matt, "you met up with him?"

"I sure did."

"What are you saying?" Conway demanded. "Who is bringing them in, and where are they coming from?"

"They're from Nevada. Come across the mountains looking for new graze. They're scouting. If they like the place, they'll tell the folks back home, and we'll see more sheep and sheepherders around here than flies on a bull's ass, come summertime. This could be just the beginning."

"Jesus," Matt said softly. "We could be getting ourselves right in the middle of a range war."

"And don't forget the noble red man," Windy said. "He will be after our ass too. We will be in the middle of a sweet threesome."

A grim silence fell while Windy worked his chew.

Finally the scout said, "I didn't get around to tellin' you about the head sheepherder."

"Who is he?"

"I can't pernounce his name," Windy said. "They call 'emselves Basques."

"Basques!" said Conway.

"They explained it to me. They ain't Spaniards, and they ain't French neither, though they come from a place between them two countries. But they been living in Nevada and growing woollies this good while. Still,

13

you'll have a helluva time trying to understand their language. Worse'n Sioux or any of them others."

"It's an old language," Conway said. "Ancient."

"I've heard it was older than Latin," Matt said, "and a whole lot more difficult."

"You mentioned their leader," Conway said.

"Like I say, he's got a name I can't pernounce, but he looks to be somethin' between a bull moose and a mountain lion; and I wouldn't be surprised if there wasn't a touch of rattlesnake there too."

Windy paused, then said, "I have heard of those Basque fellers before. You don't push 'em. They're easygoing like this feller I'm telling you about; they like to sing and dance and drink and all that. But, well..."

"How many are they?"

"I counted twelve." Windy sniffed, moving his chew to his other cheek. "They got Spencers. I seen this head feller handle that weapon. When I told him there was liable to be hostiles not appreciatin' them sheep comin' into what they consider their country he took out a deck of cards and picked one and set it up a little ways away from us, 'bout from here to the sergeant's desk out yonder." Windy paused. "He set it up *sideways*. I was a mite impressed when he hit the edge of that card with his first shot." He sniffed again and looked at the cuspidor, but didn't let fly. Instead he said, "Only person I ever seed that could shoot that good is myself."

14

two ──────────────────────────

The hard mountain trail, blown clear of the late spring snowfall, rang under the sharp hooves of the sheep. They were a full flock and more, led by Carlo, a big bellwether merino with milky eyes.

Strung out in a long line, they moved slowly up toward the rimrock. At the rear of the long train were six pack-mules and a small donkey. The mules were piled high with tents, bedrolls, food and clothing, cooking utensils, sheep hooks, and salt troughs—and plenty of ammunition for the Spencer repeaters. The donkey carried a special load: two barrels of red Basque wine.

The animals were led by men on foot, and there were other men, twelve in all. Far ahead of the lead sheep, a big man, also afoot, plodded carefully up the trail, muttering, his sharp brown eyes searching the way ahead.

Like all sheepherders, he spoke frequently to himself, for he was much alone; and when not speaking to himself, he spoke to his dog, his sheep, or even to the sky or the grass. At this moment, Otio Esteban was speaking to the magnificent snowcapped mountain peak that had suddenly come into his view as he rounded a bend in the trail.

"My God," he said, and closed his eyes for a moment.

Opening his eyes again, he looked at the gigantic white peak before him, framed in the deep blue sky. "And beyond," he said, "are there others? And beyond those, even more?"

Now his eyes dropped to Moro, his oldest dog, and

he said, "Is it not beautiful, Moro?" and tousled the animal's ears.

Otio was still far ahead of the bellwether. He had reached the summit of the rimrock, and he stood there, his breath sawing in the thin morning air. He was not unused to the mountains; indeed he had been raised in the Pyrenees, and he knew the Sierras. He stood now beneath the great cloudless sky, with the powdery snow swirling about his legs, feeling his breath moving all through his body.

Otio Esteban leaned for a moment on his *makhila*, though he was surely not a man who needed a walking stick. He kept it because it had been his father's and because it could serve as a club when the need arose. His Spencer rifle was slung over his shoulder. Turning to survey the entire horizon, Otio appeared enormous in his loose clothing, and yet he moved with the grace and swiftness of a mountain cat. Using whistles and hand signals, he ordered Moro to gather together the white-faced ewes that were strung out behind them. The animal raced away, barking to the other dogs and to the sheep, who began to respond instantly. Moro, they knew, was as tough as his master.

Ah, it was something! Otio's dark brown eyes washed across the morning sky, moving down to the layers of white mountains on the horizon, then closer down to the long valley sweeping below, with the river racing through cottonwood and box elder, roaring and swollen with the great melting snows.

"Will the *ardiak* like it?" asked the short, heavy-shouldered man who now joined him. He was an older man with bushy black eyebrows, a thick graying mustache, and a red face. He had turned his cat-green eyes to the valley.

"That indeed is the question," Otio said, not moving

16

his eyes from the scene below them. "It is always what the sheep will like, is it not so?"

The other man nodded. "It is not Nevada," he said. His name was Ciriaco; he was Otio's uncle on his mother's side, a man of sixty, very supple in his movement, and famous among the Basques for his mimicry.

"No, Uncle, it is not Nevada, but assuredly it is beautiful."

"Nor is it the Pyrenees. It is not green like the Pyrenees," insisted Ciriaco.

"Yet it is windy. And it is the wind, so Father Casimiro told, that blows away the snow in winter so the animals can feed. As we can see," Otio added, stamping his feet and letting the humor come into his eyes as he turned to the older man.

Ciriaco looked at his nephew, now thirty years old; he admired the lines of his sister's nose, his brother-in-law's firm jaw, and those big, able hands that could fight like a mountain lion and be tender too.

Looking at those hands, Ciriaco remembered them beating big Baptiste to a pulp last Fourth of July, when Otio had caught him bullwhipping a horse to its knees.

Baptiste Ferrano was known all over for his temper, and when, leaving the party on the Fourth, his sorrel had thrown him, he had beaten the animal mercilessly. Seeing it, the children ran screaming into the house to call the grownups. Otio had been the first to reach the scene.

"Baptiste!" Otio's voice had cut like a knife. But the huge man did not stop. He was beside himself with fury as his arm rose and fell, cutting the blacksnake whip across the sorrel's head.

In one bound, Otio reached him, and with one blow he smashed the giant to the ground. The horse screamed again, jerking back on its halter rope, snapping it to fall over on its rump.

Baptiste charged to his feet and Otio smashed him in the jaw, knocking him down. The big man struggled to his hands and knees. It was then that Otio picked up the whip.

"Get out, you lousy bastard! Never show yourself here again!" And he laid the bullwhip across Baptiste's back. The big man screamed. But Otio was remorseless. Again the whip smashed him on the buttocks, the shoulders. And he began to run. Another cut of the whip brought him to his knees; and he turned, blood streaming from his face, to beg.

"Please . . . please . . . Otio . . . please!"

Otio stood with his legs apart, his eyes afire, his chest heaving, not so much from physical exertion as from anger.

"The horse didn't beg, you lousy son of a goat!" And Otio threw the whip at Baptiste and then turned and walked back into the house.

Ciriaco was pulled back from his thoughts when his nephew spoke. Otio was still studying the land below them, nodding his head in approval at the vast panorama.

"It is not unlike our country, I think," he declared. "It resembles *Euzkadi*. Only it is bigger. So much bigger than the country of the Basques. No?"

"Will the *ardiak* think it beautiful?" Ciriaco asked, for he had pretty much a one-track mind. "Is it sheep country?"

Moro and the other dogs had brought the band of sheep to a stop, and they were bunched tightly on top of the rimrock overlooking the valley and the great mountains beyond.

"Nor are there many sheep here," Otio went on, ignoring Ciriaco's remark, and in continuance of his own line of thought. "Maybe there are even none. At any rate, it is what the man with the fringes told us."

18

"The army man. The scout." Ciriaco chuckled, suddenly assuming a lanky, loose posture as he puckered up his face and stuck his tongue deep into his cheek as though carrying a wad of tobacco. Now he spat and said, "Yup. They hain't no woollies in the whole of this here part of the Wyoming Territory, I'll allow." Ciriaco, who spoke good English, was a wonderful mimic, and now the two of them broke into roaring laughter over his imitation of Windy Mandalian—accent, gestures, posture, chewing, and all.

"Ah, it is good to laugh, Uncle." Otio slapped the older man affectionately on the shoulder. "The army is down there, according to what the scout told us."

Ciriaco said nothing. He was in agreement with Otio on all of it, but his enthusiasm sometimes ripened slowly, though his sense of humor was swift as an arrow. His nephew, on the other hand, was often impulsive. Where Otio was quick to temper and kindness, and would drive himself and others to the limit, Ciriaco was patient nearly to a fault. Perhaps his great sense of humor gave him a view of the world where he could see both sides of things.

Ciriaco said, "And one must not forget the Indians."

"No," Otio agreed. "One must not."

"But we will meet with the soldiers, will we not? That is what the scout said we must do."

Otio's eyes were very dark, and now suddenly they showed a light in them and his wide face opened into a great smile of affection for his uncle. It was characteristic of him to sweep on to his next mood or thought without answering. "Uncle, life is hard, no matter where a man lays his head." And he pounded his uncle on the back, causing that solid man to take a step forward to maintain his balance. They both burst into a shout of laughter and, throwing themselves into each other's arms, started to dance around in a circle.

Otio's sparkling eyes swept across the band of sheep, searching out the other men who were coming up from the rear.

"Julio!" he called out.

"Over there," someone shouted. "Behind Michel and Little Marc."

"Bravo!" Otio waved at Julio, who had been leading the gray donkey. "He is carrying the most valuable cargo in our party," he said laughingly to Ciriaco. "We must watch over him carefully!"

Grinning, Julio, a young man not yet twenty, brought the donkey up toward where the two men were standing.

"Look!" cried Otio, sweeping his hand to the horizon in a wide arc. "Drink in the miracle of the sparkling world!"

The others stopped in their tracks and looked up at the sky and at the great white shoulders of the mountains that ringed them.

"Do you see it now at last?" cried Otio.

"Ah, yes, we see it."

"Julio, bring the *xahakua,* for we must celebrate this marvelous thing."

Julio was already approaching with the goatskin wine bag.

Now the party of twelve sat on the bare, hard ground and broke bread and drank from the *xahakua.*

"A feast!" laughed Otio, lowering the *xahakua* and wiping his beard, on which several wine drops had been glistening in the light of the sun. "A feast for—what?" He looked around at his companions. "For whom?" His eyes danced.

"For love," Michel said.

"For the *ardiak!*"

"A feast for our homeland."

Otio raised the wineskin. For a moment he was motionless, and then he said very quietly, "For our Father. For God." And he drank and passed the *xahakua* to the others.

They drank and they ate mutton jerky and cheese and garlic. And presently some of the older men began to tell stories. And the sun grew warmer as it reached the top of the sky and began to descend.

Otio did not let them remain too long. "We will go to the soldiers," he said, "and they will tell us where there is a good place—and where the Indians are, so we will not go there."

He stood up, signaling the dogs. In a few moments they had crossed over to where the trail led down into the valley.

As they descended from the rimrock toward the valley, they did not see the two Brulé warriors watching them from a small stand of pine.

Suddenly it had grown warm. Suddenly it was spring with the promise of summer in the softening land, in the changing colors, in the touch of the wind. The little town, lying three hours' ride due east of Outpost Number Nine, lay indolent under the white noon sun.

It wasn't much past noon when the four men from Easy Company—Malone, Stretch Dobbs, Reb McBride, and the new recruit, Billy Golightly, reached town and tied their horses to the hitch rail in front of the Silver Tip saloon.

The Silver Tip was most of the town, though there were two other drinking establishments, a sort of hotel, a couple of eateries, a general merchandise store, and a barbershop with bathing facilities; and that was about it. The Silver Tip drew the trade, though now, with the expected Texas cattle and the hope that more herds would follow, the First Chance and the Star hoped to turn a profit.

"It ain't Denver and it ain't K.C. and it sure as hell is not Frisco," Reb McBride announced for the benefit of young Billy Golightly. "But it also ain't Tipi Town, neither. There's whiskey and, uh, women—of a sort," he added. And his companions laughed.

Stretch Dobbs, who towered easily over all the other men of Easy, exaggerated a stoop as he entered the swinging doors of the Silver Tip, saying as he did so, "It beats soldiering."

The others had followed him across the wooden boardwalk and into the dark, gloomy saloon, which smelled of beer, whiskey, tobacco, and the stale sweat of men.

In the low-ceilinged room, Stretch almost had to duck his head to avoid striking the thick crossbeams. "Place is made for midgets," he muttered.

The customers were not numerous: a couple of sourdough types at a corner table, three or four old-timers tilting back in their chairs along the far wall, three men who looked to be cowhands at the far end of the bar, and some nondescript locals and maybe a transient or two around the potbellied stove in the center of the room.

The floor slanted; the floorboards themselves were uneven, bringing to mind again some old-timer's remark that the town had been nailed together in about a week. And the floor was well marked with spittle, and scarred from matches, lighted cigar butts, and general scuffing. Along the customer's side of the bar stood three reeking spittoons. Some others were spotted about the premises, though none at the stove, the sport being to spit onto the red-hot metal.

The visitors from Easy Company stood at the bar while the proprietor, on the sober side of the bar—actually a pair of boards supported by trestles—placed glasses and a bottle of whiskey before them. From the wall behind the proprietor's round shoulders, the battered head of a bull elk blindly surveyed the clientele, both its glass eyes having been shot out.

Malone loosened his shirt and belt, and McBride followed suit, and now both of them turned around and leaned back with their elbows on the bar to look at the room.

Although the jumbo stove was not lighted, the group of locals stood close to it, still wearing coats and, of course, hats, for while it was spring and a warm day, they were still in their winter ways.

"By God, it's as dark as a man's pocket in here," Stretch Dobbs observed, peering into his glass of whiskey.

"Shit, a man can't rightly see what he's drinkin'," Billy Golightly said.

"Be damn glad you can't," the bartender-proprietor declared. He was a round man with round shoulders and a very round face; like a ball. He wore a belt as well as suspenders, and had a sorrowful expression on his face. He was totally bald, the dome of his large white head sweating a bit. His name was Roy Skinner.

Billy Golightly chuckled at that. He was pleased that the men had asked him to come along. He knew the others thought him shy, for he never talked about himself or his family or where he'd come from. He looked so young that the word had gotten around that probably he had lied about his age in order to enlist.

Right now he was leaning on the bar, listening to Private Malone, who was garrulous as always, even when not under the influence. The big Irishman was telling one of his endless stories. At length, finishing his tortuous account of some mishap, he belched abruptly and

23

stepped back from the bar, raising his glass as he did so. At the same time his other hand touched the butt of the Schofield model Smith & Wesson at his waist. Putting down his glass, he let his drinking hand fall to his second gun, a Deane & Adams, and he hoisted the belt and both holsters, bent his knees slightly, and, reaching down, scratched deep into his crotch.

"Been meaning to ask how come you and some of the others pack two sets of hardware," Billy said, nodding toward the armament at Malone's waist. "I only got issued the one."

"Bought it," Malone said. "Noticed Lieutenant Kincaid, have you? He's carrying a Scoff and a Colt to boot."

"Pretty fancy-looking," Billy said with a smile. "And he looks like he can really handle those irons."

"That he can," Reb McBride said. "what say we try nosing our way to the bottom of another glass of this here wicked juice?"

"Soldier, that is a dumb question. My aim in visiting this bustling city is to partake of all the alcohol I can hold." Stretch raised his eyes toward the top of his own head, and lowered them down his long front, while his companions broke into guffaws of laughter.

"That'll surely take a peck of drinking," said Reb.

"Well, by God, looky here now!" A big voice broke from the gloom at the end of the bar where the three cowboys were drinking. "Looky here—if it ain't the little soldier boys livin' it up!"

Malone, in the act of raising his glass, didn't skip a beat, the glass continuing to his lips. Beside him, Billy Golightly was aware of a slight change in the big Irishman's vibration. And now all at once the room was really quiet.

Now a new voice came from the group at the end of

the bar. "What you kids doin', drinkin' in a man's parlor, huh?"

Malone set his glass down firmly on the wood planking. He spoke without turning his head, keeping his eyes right on the row of bottles behind the bar. "Why, we just thought we might be findin' ourselves a good place to take a piss," he said softly, though all could clearly hear him. "We didn't figger there'd be all this baby shit to be steppin' into."

"You know who you're talkin' to, Yank?"

"Sounds like Texas to me, boys," Reb said, speaking suddenly and fast. "Shit, fellers, let's take it slow. Me, I'm from Sweetwater, down in God's country."

"Then what in hell for did you sell your ass to a passel of Union shitheads!" said the third man, who had not previously spoken.

Stretch Dobbs stepped back from the bar. "Mister, what's the problem? We're just in here for some of the tasty water. Whyn't you join us?"

By now, two men had drifted over to the cowboys from the stove, and another had come in the door, making six.

"Circle Box men, soldier boy, is fussy who they drink with. What we would like to know is why you soldier boys ain't out protectin' Circle Box cattle, which is what you are getting paid to do."

"You got it wrong, sir," Malone said. "We are gettin' paid with government money—just to come in here and drink and lay the girls and raise us some hell."

The Texan was big. He had hands like saddles, and he stepped away from the bar and faced Malone and the other men of Easy Company.

"Listen, you son of a bitch, do you know who you're talkin' to?"

The Irishman, two hundred pounds soaking wet, detached himself from his companions and stood facing the Texan. "I don't know *who* I'm talkin' to, but I know *what;* and you better turn around so I can talk to your face and not your asshole."

"Now, boys, men...let's ease it. I'm buying a round." It was Roy Skinner, the baldheaded proprietor of the Silver Tip, placing a full bottle on the bar.

The Texans had now drifted deeper into the room, while the local customers faded into the background. Six Texans to four soldiers, Malone was thinking, and decided Easy Company had the advantage.

Nobody had responded to the barkeep's offer of free booze, and the proprietor eyed his row of bottles in back of the bar nervously. He was glad he had not replaced the big mirror after the time a shotgun blast from a cut-down Greener .12-gauge had wiped it off the wall.

The big Texan was real close to the soldiers now, and suddenly his head whipped around to young Billy Golightly.

"What the hell you starin' at, little boy?" he barked.

"Just looking at that big hogleg you got there in that holster, mister. No offense." Billy's voice was as innocent as that of a small child caught with his hand in the cookie jar.

"I didn't know they took kids for soldiers in the Union army." And the cowboy threw back his head and laughed. "Give the little feller a drink," the Texan said suddenly to Skinner, without looking at him. "Fill the glass. I mean, fill 'er!"

The proprietor poured, and the cowboy pushed the glass toward Billy Golightly. It was full to the brim with whiskey. "Drink it," he said.

The room was without a sound as Billy Golightly reached for the glass.

"It'll kill him sure," one of the cowboys said.

26

"Hey, what's that?" said Malone, pointing down at the floor right by the big Texan's boots.

The cowboy's eyes dropped, and the big Irishman nailed him squarely on the jaw. The Texan staggered, his knees folded, and he went down grabbing Malone around the legs. At the same moment the man standing next to him picked up a chair and smashed the Irishman over the head with it, to no effect.

Stretch Dobbs hit Malone's assailant with a rabbit punch right behind his ear, but the cowboy, tall and thin just like Stretch, didn't drop as he should have, but turned, and now the pair whaled away at each other, looking like a couple of huge, lethal spiders. Finally, Stretch connected and his opponent dropped, but promptly rose and, grabbing the same chair that had struck Malone, smashed it into Stretch's crotch. Dobbs fell to his knees, cursing and in agony.

Meanwhile, McBride was battling a thickset man with arms as big as the bugler's legs, and Billy Golightly was brought down by a flying bottle.

Malone, having knocked two men flat, was suddenly confronted by a brace of cowboys, one diving at his knees and bringing him to the floor, the other immediately jumping on his head.

But the Irishman's head was as hard as his temper, and in a moment he had twisted to his knees, risen, and elbowed one of his assailants in the crotch and kicked the other in the kidney.

Billy Golightly had staggered to his feet only to be driven to the floor and into oblivion with a barrage of lefts and rights from one of the cowboys. His conqueror did not taste victory for more than an instant, however, for Malone smashed him at the base of his spine with a hamlike fist, and then chopped him beautifully on the back of the neck; he fell as though poleaxed.

27

Suddenly two shots rang out, and a hard voice broke through the din of battle. "That will be all, you sons of bitches!"

It was Ching Domino, standing in the doorway with a sixgun in each hand. The room was instantly silent.

Malone was the only combatant on his feet. "Who the hell are you?" he demanded.

"If you didn't have that uniform on, I'd show you, mister!"

"Good to find you in such a sociable mood," Billy Golightly gasped as he pulled himself painfully to his feet.

"Put them guns away and I'll teach you to respect the United States Mounted Infantry," Malone said. One eye, already a very dark purple, was closing rapidly. Blood laced the side of his jaw.

Ching Domino chuckled without mirth, holstering his weapons. "Another time, mister. Not now. I ain't drawing on the army. I'm only here to get my men back to work. And why don't you and your buddies there get your asses into your saddles and protect our cattle, like your blue-assed captain said you would."

Malone was about to take a step forward and settle it right there, but Dobbs grabbed his leg, pulling himself to his feet. "Let the fuckers go. We beat 'em, Malone."

"You men, get on your horses and haul ass. I mean right now!" And Ching Domino spat hard on the floor. He stood still now, staring at Billy Golightly. "Ain't I seen you somewheres?"

"Right here," Billy said.

"Who's gonna pay the damages?" cried Roy Skinner, rubbing his hands across the top of his bald head as he came from behind the bar. "Look at this place. It's a wreck!"

"Our sergeant will talk to you," Malone said. "Don't worry about it."

"He better, by God," said Skinner. "He damn well better!"

"I said don't worry about it."

They were all on their feet now, the Circle Box men staggering out after Ching Domino, and the men from Easy Company following Malone.

Stretch Dobbs felt his jaw to see if it was still in place. "The sarge is gonna be real pleased to see us, Malone," he said.

Malone didn't answer, but turned to Billy Golightly. "Say, kid, what were you gonna do with that full glass of whiskey, when that big son of a bitch told you to drink it. That could've killed you!"

"Why, I was going to drink it," Billy said innocently.

"Drink it! Jesus!"

"I like whiskey," Billy said. "Besides, it was free."

three ─────────────

It seemed the yellow flowers and bluebirds were everywhere. In the timber and in the draws there were elk and pronghorn antelope and mule deer; and there were still some buffalo. In the horse herd, spotted colts tried their spindly new legs, and one could hear the tinkle of the grazing bells. It was a good sign, the old people said, yet they spoke carefully, for the times in general were hard.

There had been no fighting with the white soldiers for a while, the one bad thing being the slaying of Young Man Catching Up. Much sorrow had fallen on the people, with keening and cutting oneself, for Young Man had been a promising warrior, young, proud, and strong like his brother Quick Thunder and their cousin Wound. Anger and bitterness had run high in the camp of the Brulés, and though the bad moment was not spoken of as it had been, it stayed in the hearts of everyone, for Young Man Catching Up had not been killed in battle but through treachery, shot in the back by one of the Gray Men, those the whites called outlaws. Quick Thunder and Wound had sworn revenge on the whites, and only the stature of Little Hawk, himself a warrior who had fought with Crazy Horse, had kept them and the other young warriors from attacking the whites.

Now, just at the end of the Moon of the New Grass, the Brulés, only one sleep away from the white soldiers, were at peace. The young men still smoldered for revenge, but Little Hawk and the elders of the council had insisted that it was foolishness to attack all the whites because of Young Man. Besides, the soldier Kincaid had come to the camp and told them that he and his friend Windy would find the Gray Man and punish him.

Thus the band of Little Hawk had been making no fighting, just going out for meat because there was so little to eat at the agency, and the winter had been cold and long. Still, no one was coming in with white men's scalps.

With the moon growing again, the land awakening to the summertime, the people were ready to hunt; the older ones hoped that a big hunt would ease the restlessness of the young warriors.

This day had broken gently over the Brulé camp, the sun slipping over the tipis, pausing on the cottonwood and crackwillow in the draws that ran through the surrounding prairie. Much of the rolling prairie was greening. But not for long. Soon the sea of grass would turn to its more familiar tawny brown. But next year, the old ones predicted, there would be less buffalo, less game to fill the parfleches...

A group of boys from five to seven were playing at war, different bands of them fighting each other with mud balls that they threw with yellow sticks. The bigger boys played a game called Throwing Them Off Their Horses. Usually it was played with real horses, but these days the larger boys were the "horses" carrying smaller boys on their backs, who grappled with the "enemy horsemen," trying to unseat them. It was a rough game, good wrestling, building strong arms and legs, strong wind, and a quick attentiveness for whatever lay ahead.

In the lodge of Little Hawk, a half-dozen headmen sat with their chief in council. The men had entered the lodge carefully, paying attention to all the details necessary to the occasion and the person of him who was their chosen leader. They had seated themselves in the required order, and they had smoked, sending the pipe around the circle in the prescribed manner.

"It is good," Little Hawk said.

"*Heya,*" said the others.

"What of the news brought by Sees Far Off and Mole?" asked the young warrior Quick Thunder. He was the youngest man in the lodge, and though he often spoke out angrily against the whites, speaking for war to the finish, he often found favor in Little Hawk's eyes, who remembered himself as a young man with the same anger.

A murmur touched the circle of older warriors now. The two scouts, Sees Far Off and Mole, had brought news of the sheep and the herder men with the repeating rifles, seen not more than a day's ride away, just in the Absarokas. Sees Far Off and Mole had been visiting relatives in the Oglala camp near the Piney River, and it was on their way back to the Brulé camp that they had seen the men who spoke with the strange tongue, and the many woolly animals.

"They are coming into the country fast, it is certain," a warrior named Old Face said, moving his eagle-wing fan. "If not right here where we are now, then close, close enough to touch."

Weasel, an older man, now spoke. "But they will not come on this land. This land has been given us by Washtone."

At his words, Quick Thunder's eyes flashed. "It is not Washtone's land to give," he said harshly. And then he paused, feeling Little Hawk's eyes on him.

"It is good to remember how to speak in council," the chief said.

"Forgive me, Grandfather," Quick Thunder said, and turned to the man known as Weasel. "I spoke in anger against the whites, Grandfather, not against him who

33

taught me many things, not only in my youth, but still in this moment."

"It is well," Weasel said.

"It is the man who is angry that will lose everything," Little Hawk said.

"But what can be done?" Wound, who had been silent thus far, spoke up. "Can we go on being fed rotten food, being lied to, being treated like prisoners in our own land? It is an angry question, but a sorrowful one too."

"These men let their cattle and sheep go everywhere," another warrior said. He was a man with many wrinkles in his face, but his body was straight as he sat impassive, listening. Now he spoke slowly, but with a good strength, the strength of conviction. His name was Running Fast. "Now, with the cattle in the south and the sheep from the west . . . it means there will be more. And they will surely kill and drive away the game, of which there is little enough now."

"With the sheep of the white man, the grass is not fit for our horses to eat once they have passed over it. And so now even our ponies will starve," said another young warrior, named He-in-His-Lodge.

Now Old Face spoke again, saying, "These *Wasichus* will bring more, more will follow in their steps. And they will kill what little remain of the buffalo."

"*Heya,*" the others said. "It is so."

The lodge was silent and the pipe was passed again, each one smoking, grave with the thoughts that held them all.

It was so. There were so many things. The rations, the having to ask permission for everything, even to hunt; and now the cattle people and those with the sheep.

Now Little Hawk spoke. "It is as it is," he said. "We can fight the *Wasichus* and we will be killed. With honor," he added, looking at the three young warriors—

Quick Thunder, his cousin Wound, and He-in-His-Lodge. "But the *Wasichus* are many more than the Brulés, many more than all the tribes together. It will no longer be as it was at the Greasy Grass against Yellow Hair. The *Wasichus* are more than the blades of grass. And they do not fight as the Lakota do. They wish to rub out everything. We must survive. What is important is that our people live. If we fight, the *Wasichus* will kill us all; and there will be none left of our entire nation."

"It is true the whites never stop killing." Quick Thunder said. "That is all the soldiers do. Where are their families, their old ones, their children?"

"But what can be done?" Running Fast asked.

A long silence fell.

Finally, Little Hawk spoke. "We must talk to the soldiers," he said, and he watched the anger leap into the eyes of Quick Thunder, Wound, and He in His Lodge. Yet they said no more.

When they had gone, he cleaned his pipe and filled it. Then, offering it, he prayed.

All that night, Little Hawk sat in his blanket, not moving even when Rising Moon, his youngest wife, brought something for him to eat. These days there was much to trouble the heart; the young men were always pushing to fight the whites, and he knew that except for his own standing as a warrior, and the respect he commanded, there would have been an open break in the camp.

Little Hawk felt sorry for the young men. Once he had been the same. He was surely no paper chief, and they knew this. And the young men listened to him. For the moment. But they were giving in to their impatience. It was a bad sign.

They said it was better to die a man than live in chains in the white man's iron house, or be held prisoner on the land he has stolen, the land for which he has no love, but only hatred.

Ah, yes. Only what of the younger ones, the children, those that were even now at their mothers' breasts? What would happen to them, to the old people, to the Lakota Nation itself, if all fought to the death?

It was much to trouble the heart. Well, he would ride to a high place and build a lodge and purify himself with the heat from the special fire. Maybe then he could cry for a vision; maybe then he could dream. For he must see what was the good road for the people. It was not possible to act truly from himself, for he was weak and could not see. The true road for the people could only be seen from what was Above.

At last he saw the morning star come into the sky, and when the sun rose, Rising Moon brought his horse, and he rode out of camp on the magnificent silver-maned buckskin. He rode alone. He rode with his body as straight as an arrow. He rode in silence.

"It was him."

"You sure? How can you be sure?"

"Elihu, I am telling you it was him."

"But can you be sure?"

"I swear it was him. I seen him that close."

"Jesus . . ." Cohoes stared across the table at his fore-man.

The interior of the Silver Tip in the early morning was deserted save for the two men at the corner table, the baldheaded Roy Skinner reading a month-old news-paper behind the bar, and the old swamper who was carrying out empties. Outside a soft rain was falling, the first rain in several days, and the room smelled damp.

After a moment, Cohoes's grainy voice broke in. "Thing is, did he recognize you?"

36

"You're talking about—"

"Who else!" Cohoes cut in irritably. "Hogan, that's who I'm talkin' about, not your grandmother! Or whatever he calls himself. I don't reckon he's callin' himself Hogan in the army." He leaned forward, his eyes piercing the man across the table. "You *sure?*"

"I am not shittin' you, Elihu. Hell, you know me better'n that, for Chrissakes."

Cohoes's voice was as forbidding as his face as he looked at his foreman plumb center. "That's the point, Domino, I do know you better than that." And, holding his foreman with his hard eyes, he raised his glass again and drank, his eyes still on Ching Domino as he put down the tumbler.

Cohoes could see that Domino didn't like it; but he wanted it that way. Every so often he found it necessary to rein in the big gunslinger. Ching Domino had his uses, but thinking clearly was not one of them. He could handle men, though, rough men, and his gun was swift. The thing was, now and again he'd get uppity.

"Maybe pretty soon we'll make our play with the army—if we have to," Cohoes said.

"How would that be?" Ching Domino wrinkled his thick forehead. "What kind of play with the army?"

"If I don't get the cooperation I'm askin' for, I might need a little extra, like the true identity of one of their men. Because you can bet the last hair on your ass, not only don't they know who he is, but they'd give plenty to land Larrabee Hogan." He was staring past Ching Domino as he spoke, his eyes half closed.

"Hogan must know by now what happened to his cattle," Domino said.

"*His* cattle?"

"What he took to be his."

"That's better." Cohoes canted his head at his foreman

now for emphasis. "More than likely how come he busted out of the pen."

Ching Domino grinned. "We'll be ready for him," he said.

"*You* will be ready for him," Cohoes said, and the emphasis on "you" was not light.

Ching Domino was a tough man. He knew it, and everyone acquainted with him knew it. But he didn't like the way Elihu Cohoes looked at him right now. At the same time, he had never been able to explain to himself why Cohoes never went armed, and why so many people were careful in his presence, Domino included.

"He must be a good bit younger—the kid, I'm meaning," he said now, to ease the moment for himself.

"A bullet is a bullet, no matter if a baby pulls the trigger," Cohoes said, getting to his feet. "You keep a close eye on it. We'll more'n likely run into that kid brother again."

Ching Domino pushed back his chair, running the back of his hairy hand across his mouth. "When you figger the herd to move?"

"We'll see about the escort first. I don't aim to risk anything with them Injuns all pissed off." He sniffed. "Now then, till we move 'em, we'll let 'em feed and pick up the weight they lost on the drive. That grama grass ought to do 'er."

Ching Domino's face moved suddenly, and Cohoes realized he was grinning.

"Don't worry," the cattleman said. "I don't expect my foreman to know feed and stock. I got Haines for that."

"Right," Domino said. "Your foreman don't have to, when he knows this." And his middle finger touched the holstered handgun at his right thigh.

Unwittingly, not realizing he was doing so, Ching Domino had dropped his eyes to his companion's belt, where there were no guns. Catching himself, he brought his eyes up to find Elihu Cohoes staring right at him.

"Maybe," Cohoes said, again canting his head at his foreman. "Maybe someday you might even get good enough with that there peashooter where you don't have to carry it at all."

And he turned and walked out of the saloon.

four ———————

"So it's the four of you, is it?" Sergeant Ben Cohen, seated massively behind his desk in the Easy Company orderly room, surveyed the battered countenances of Malone, Dobbs, McBride, and Golightly.

"Sarge, it wasn't our fault." Stretch Dobbs spoke carefully, trying to work his words around the bruises and cuts on his mouth, the pain in his jaw. "Those damn cow-holes started the whole goddamn thing."

"Bullshit."

Dobbs's left eye popped, the right one being totally closed. "Sarge—"

"We was mindin' our own business, Sergeant," Reb McBride started to put in.

"Bullshit."

"Sarge, we beat the hell out of them fuckers. They insulted the uniform, Sarge, that's what started the trouble." Malone spoke strongly as always, even though there was a large blue lump on his jaw, and his left ear looked like a mangled potato.

"Bullshit."

Sergeant Ben Cohen, the first soldier of Easy Company, sat like a statue of Solomon, his imperial eyes examining the four wretches who stood in varying degrees of distress—physical and otherwise—before the judicial desk. Like Conway and Kincaid, Cohen too was over age in grade. But unlike Conway and Kincaid, Ben Cohen did not suffer in silence. He said nothing in front of the men, but his wife Maggie knew the song backwards and forwards and inside-out.

Now, having delivered his considered, succinct, and wholly colorful appraisal of the passage-at-arms in town, the first sergeant leaned his thick forearms on his desk and said, "By the look of you, Malone, I'd have to say you didn't do much to uphold the honor of the United States Army of the West."

"Sarge, we won. There was six of them, and only four of us. We beat the shit outta them . . ."

The hard eyes swept the four miscreants like a couple of Gatling guns.

"And, uh—the damage?" The thick forehead now creased in sudden innocence, the voice grew softer. "Who, pray tell, is paying for the damage to Mr. Skinner's establishment?" As that enormously muscled body leaned back, the chair creaked loudly; but the sergeant only raised his eyes to the ceiling, lips pursed, fingers laced across that great chest as he revolved his thumbs. The exemplification of magisterial patience, the Master suffered himself to listen.

A moment passed in which if a feather had fallen it would have been heard.

"Might the first soldier of this organization—this organization which feeds you, clothes you, protects you from wild Indians and, when it can, wild women and other terrors of the frontier—might he ask you . . ." And he leaned forward swift as silk, his jaws opening like a slashing grizzly as the words crashed into the four hapless defenders of Easy Company's honor. ". . . just who the hell is going to pay for your fucking wreckage!"

The force of the explosion drove the four backward.

Sergeant Cohen rose like a wall of fire to his feet, and stood there glaring at each one in turn, as though the very force of his eyes would drag an answer out of the culprits.

Billy Golightly had never experienced anything like it, and he began to sniff nervously.

"Don't sniff at me, goddammit, Golightly!"

"Sarge..." Malone shifted on his feet, trying to mollify the awesome presence standing in front of them.

"Ah, and wouldn't you know... wouldn't you just know it... that right in the middle of it all is—guess who? The Malone! The Malone himself, in person. By God, and is it himself is going to pay?"

"Sarge... we thought... the slush fund..."

"What! The slush fund for you dumb bastards breaking up a whole entire saloon! The rest of the company is going to pay for what you done? By God!" He dropped into his chair, stricken with disbelief.

They stood there trying not to show their discomfort, for fear of drawing a further outburst.

Suddenly those fearsome eyes swiveled to young Billy Golightly.

"Golightly..."

"Yes, Sarge?"

"I hope you have learned a lesson about who not to associate with in this man's army."

"Yes, Sarge."

"What have you learned?"

Billy Golightly looked totally nonplussed. He wanted more than anything else to reach up and scratch his head, but the look on Ben Cohen's face forbade any such indulgence.

"Dammit, Golightly, I asked you a question. What have you learned?"

"I learned... I learned a lesson about who to associate with in this man's army. Uh, I mean, who *not* to associate with, Sarge."

Dobbs, McBride, and Malone looked as though they were going to burst. And so did Sergeant Cohen, although in his case, it was not from laughter.

"Now I know where you come from," he said, his eyes boring into his target, who had answered him out

43

of pure innocence. "You are one of those people who knows a lot. One of those who can tell what'll happen tomorrow, next year. You know ahead of time what's going to happen to all of us."

"Why, no, Sarge."

"I mean anyone so goddamn fucking smart has got to be able to tell the future." The big head swung across the group as the eyes searched for any movement in the direction of humor. "And what would the Malone say to this?"

"I'd say the sergeant was right, Sarge."

"That Golightly here can tell us what's gonna happen?"

"That's right, Sarge."

"So, Golightly . . . tell us what is going to happen to the four of you."

Billy Golightly began to perspire.

"I will help you." And Sergeant Cohen opened his desk drawer and brought out a stack of spoons. Counting out four, he placed them with their handles toward the four miscreants. "Tell, Golightly."

Young Billy was gray around the eyes, and he began to sniff. The nudge that Malone gave him in his bruised side almost knocked him down; but somehow he managed to get the signal as, turning, he saw the big Irishman nod toward the window.

"The spoons, Sarge."

"That's right."

"With those spoons, Sarge, we will dig."

"That is correct, Private Golightly."

"Now what will you dig?" He waited, and when nothing more was forthcoming from Golightly, he said, "Malone, you are an old hand at spoons and prediction, ain't you?"

"Yes, Sarge. Sure."

44

"Tell Golightly and the others what you will be digging."

"A perfect six-by-six-by-six, Sarge."

"That is correct." The first soldier of Easy Company straightened in his chair. "Soldiers, pick up those spoons!"

Four battered hands dove to the desk.

"And get your asses outta here and start diggin' back of the paddock. Malone knows where. By God, he's dug up half the Territory of Wyoming. Git!"

When the door had closed, Cohen sat back in his swivel chair, exhausted, wondering how in the name of whatever one could name he had ever gotten into the position of wet-nursing such a bunch of incompetent assholes.

Suddenly the door to the CO's office opened.

"Everything all right out here, Sergeant?" Conway's brisk voice seemed to be lightly laced with humor, and Cohen realized he had probably overheard some of it.

"Yes, sir, everything is fine."

"I couldn't help hearing something about cowboys in town, or something. Would that be Cohoes's men?"

Cohen quickly related the story to the captain, and with colorful effect.

Conway suppressed a smile. "I get the picture. There is plenty of resentment on the part of the cattlemen. But you know, Ben, I do not interfere in your business. I was only asking."

"Yes, sir."

"Who were the four again? Malone . . . ?"

"Malone, Dobbs, Bugler McBride, and young Billy Golightly."

"Ah, yes, I wanted to speak to you about him. He's got a really high score with the Springfield. But he looks awfully young. I mean, he looks sixteen, something like that. I suppose he's lied about his age."

"I'm thinkin' the same, Captain."

"I think it's not so unusual."

"It happens."

The captain looked at the back of his hand suddenly. "How is he?"

"He's a good man, Captain. Willing, works hard, knows horses and guns a lot better than most, and no bullshit. The men like him, sir."

"I suppose Malone has broken him in on the entertainments that are possible in town."

"So far as the saloons go, he sure has, sir. As for the women, I don't know that any of the four of them had the time or strength left to taste those pleasures, Captain."

Conway chuckled, his thoughts suddenly turning to his wife, Flora. His eyes found the clock on the orderly room wall. "I'm going over to my quarters, Sergeant. I'll be back shortly."

"Yes, sir."

With his hand on the doorknob, Conway turned. "And how is the charming and delightful Mrs. Cohen?"

"Maggie's just fine, sir. Giving me hell as usual, so I know everything's good with her."

Conway grinned, nodded, and the grin turned to a little smile at his lips as he thought of Maggie Cohen, the great Irish wife with the blue eyes and copious bosom. And this thought brought him right back to Flora Conway as he closed the door behind him.

When Warner Conway walked into his quarters, his wife called to him through the door that led to the room just off the parlor.

"Warner?"

"Yes, my dear."

"You're back early."

"Sorry, dear, shall I leave?"

"You silly. Come on in, I'm just finishing my bath."

When he walked through the door, she looked up at him from the tub in which she was almost totally immersed. The soapsuds were making mountains, and some had spilled to the floor. Her long black hair was swept onto the top of her head, and his eyes caught the most delightful ears he had ever seen in his life.

"Warner, what are you staring at?"

"Those wonderful ears."

She was superb, her face laughing, the skin soft as a baby's, her brown eyes shining at him. In her late thirties, Flora Conway looked a good bit younger. Warner Conway thought he would be madly in love with her if she were ninety.

Stepping over to the tub, he leaned down and kissed her on her full lips.

"Oh, Warner, that's very nice. Wherever did you learn to kiss like that?"

"I learned from a delightful, black-haired, brown-eyed, spanky-bottomed beauty."

"Spanky-bottomed beauty indeed!" And laughing, she began soaping herself, keeping her eyes on him as he took off his jacket.

"What did you do with this, uh, instructress, my dear?"

"Oh, we had lessons."

"Did you learn much?"

"I learned that I loved my teacher."

"Her spanky bottom?" Flora laughed aloud, and he adored the flush on her face. And she, as always, loved to tease him.

Suddenly she stood up, her firm breasts bouncing right before his eyes. Turning, she reached for her bath towel. "Will this bottom do, Captain Conway?"

Warner Conway did not answer. He was already almost totally undressed. In a moment he had her on the bed, having carried her across the room. She was still only partly dry from her bath and smelling delicious as she helped him remove the rest of his clothes.

The storm hit after dark, around ten o'clock, with rolling thunder and streaks of lightning flashing across the sky. Its suddenness was almost unnerving, even to the Basques, who were accustomed to storms.

They had made camp at dusk and were now relaxing in their tents with a little wine, some stories, and song. At the first crack of thunder they'd thought it might be rifle fire; old Xerxes even said it could be the Indians.

Now the lightning stabbing across the black sky illuminated the soaking sheep, which were huddled, cowering, against the shining ground.

Inside the wet canvas tent, Otio and Ciriaco had a small fire going. Three other men, squatting close together for warmth, smoked and watched the fire. Otio got to his feet as an especially blinding flash of lightning and sharp crack of thunder shone on the walls of the tent. Stepping outside, he took a look at the churning sky, which now ripped and crackled every few seconds. The sheep were terrified. The rain, mixed with sleet and snow, drove to the ground and onto Otio's bare head and shoulders; the cuffs of his jacket were soaking at his wrists. When he came back into the tent, he brought the dogs with him. Dripping, they sat in a semicircle, looking at the men with serious eyes.

"How is it out there?" someone asked.

"Not bad." Otio let a long sigh run through him. "We *Eskualdunak*, we Basques," he said, and again sighed, his breath forming a cloud before his face. "It is how we live, no? In the storm, in the heat, and in the soft blue days of spring and summer. And so, the bitter comes with the sweet. Is it not so?"

A sudden crash of thunder hit them like a blow, seeming as though it would tear the sky apart. Ciriaco, standing just outside the tent now, watched the flashes of blue lightning sizzle through the black, soaking night, while the thunder boomed like artillery. It was a dance, a great wall of thunder and roiling sky lit with lightning would close in on them, then retreat to regroup and weave into a new pattern and once more sweep down upon them. It was bitterly cold, and inside the tent the men crowded around the fire, and now and then the smoke made them cough.

Around one o'clock the storm stopped, quite suddenly. Silence stretched over the prairie, save for the wet sound of water dripping around the tent.

Ciriaco had already come back inside, and now Otio said, "The others must be all right, but I'll take a look all the same." And he ducked outside once again.

In a few moments he was back. "They are true Basques—not like us. They're all snoring like mothers-in-law."

The tent filled with laughter.

"True Basques, indeed," someone said. "One wonders whether they even knew there was a storm."

Gradually they fell silent. The dogs had been let out. Ciriaco lay on his back, looking up at the top of the tent. The others, save for Otio, who was sitting up, appeared to be asleep. The tent was warmer with their heavy breathing.

After a long while, Ciriaco spoke. "I have been wondering, Otio, when you will find a wife. It is time. Though it is not my business."

Otio grunted. "It is not so easy to find a mate, Uncle. Not all of us can have the good fortune that you had in finding Tante Illista."

Ciriaco smiled up at the peak of the tent, thinking of his wife of many years. "She is a good cook," he said simply. And then, "Maria was a good wife, too. But one can neither bring back nor copy the dead, Otio."

"That I know," Otio said wearily.

"Otio . . ."

"Yes, Uncle?"

"Get some sleep."

"Good night, Uncle."

After a long moment, Ciriaco said, "What do you think, Otio? Is it good for the *ardiak?*"

"I will know better tomorrow, or the next day," Otio said.

Ciriaco laughed. "You are learning, nephew. It is good."

"The man in buckskins said we must think of the Indians."

"That is certain," Ciriaco said.

There was a movement at the front of the tent, and Michel put his head in. "All is well."

"You want to sleep?" Otio asked. "I am wide awake."

"I'll watch for another hour." And they heard Michel sloshing away from the tent.

Ciriaco rolled over onto his side, a gentle snore riding the whole length of his nose.

Otio continued to sit by the fire, now and again reaching over to stir it to life. It grew colder in the tent, and he held out his hands, rubbing them over the meager heat. But he did not add more fuel. He wished he had a woman.

In the morning, he was thinking, he might go and see

the soldiers. In the morning, the sky would be clear and then they could see more of the country and how it would be for the sheep.

five _____

In the hot sun, the four diggers surveyed the territory marked off for excavation. Each carried his spoon in his hand. Glumly they looked at the small heaps of dirt that had already been dug out. Their heads ached, their bodies were sore, not only from digging, but from the encounter at the Silver Tip. Yet, though bloody, they were unbowed; all resented the injustice meted out by their first sergeant.

"Shit, we was defending the honor of the company," said Stretch Dobbs as they resumed their kneeling positions and began to dig.

"Defending the whole fucking army, by God," allowed Malone; and even though they were trying to speak low in order not to draw attention to themselves, Malone's voice resonated like the roll of a drum. Dobbs and McBride threw their eyes uneasily in the direction of the orderly room.

"Better hold it down, Malone."

"What the hell d'you mean, hold it down! I'm talking real quiet. And all I'm saying is it ain't fair. Shit, last month Wojensky got in a fight with some asshole feather merchant, and Cohen didn't do a fucking thing to him!"

"Shut up."

"Fuck off!"

"Shut up, for Chrissake, here comes Cohen now."

Swiftly the four bent closer to their work, each one working at a side of the square that had been marked off by four pieces of prairie sod. Their eyes glued to the ground, they dug. Nobody looked up, there wasn't even a glance in the direction of the approaching personification of anger, injustice, muscular power, and cunning. But all felt the trembling of the earth as the menacing boots of Sergeant Cohen came into view.

"Pretty slow digging, I'd say."

No comment greeted this deadly observation.

"I said, pretty slow digging."

Stretch Dobbs raised his head. "Oh, hello there, Sarge. Yup, we'll speed her up." And he began to dig furiously with the spoon. The others followed suit.

Sergeant Cohen watched for a few moments, his hands clasped together behind his back, his head bent in concentration as his eyes bore into the sweating laborers. When he cleared his throat, it sounded like gravel being run out of a wagon box.

"I regret to inform you men that I have very bad news for you."

This remark did cause a cessation of the digging, and the four raised their heads to regard the colossus standing directly above them.

"A pity it is," he went on, "especially for young Golightly there, who will miss the taste of true army discipline—for the moment," he added swiftly and with emphasis. "For the moment. For now, you are excused from your present detail. But if I hear of one more infraction, one more instance of your indulging in behavior not becoming a soldier, I will not only throw the book at you, but the whole fucking post!" He stood glaring at their dumbfounded surprise.

"Now move! Get off your asses and move! You're going out on patrol with Lieutenant Kincaid! It is regrettable, let me add, that we're shorthanded here, and the lieutenant has to draw upon this particular source." Without another word, without even a pause or a further glare, the sergeant turned and started back to the orderly room.

Then suddenly he barked out, without turning his head, "Clean them spoons perfect—and bring 'em to my office!"

The news brought in by the scouts that the soldiers were nearby sent a shudder through the Brulé camp. But as a sign of friendship, Little Hawk had ridden out with some of his headmen to receive the visitors. He had worn the officer hat that the Great Father had sent him long ago, and which was now laced with cricket holes, and had its top cut out both for air and for connection with the Above. Through it, a single eagle feather stood up.

Now, while the soldiers waited at a distance from the camp, Matt Kincaid and Windy Mandalian sat in the chief's lodge with Little Hawk and a half-dozen headmen, along with Quick Thunder and Wound.

The visitors had been offered the pipe of welcome, the chief filling the pipe with the tobacco for the occasion, and setting it on the buffalo chip in front of him. Then he lighted it and offered the stem to the sky and to the earth and to the four directions. When this was done, they smoked. And because they had smoked, they must only speak the truth.

"We have come to speak about the steer that was slain and butchered," Windy began. "The cattleman who owned the steer came to see Lieutenant Kincaid and Captain Conway. He was not happy."

"The steer was on reservation land," Little Hawk said. "And we have talked of it. The white man must not have his animals here."

"*Ho!*" The voices rose around the circle at the chief's words.

"Why did you not drive the steer back?" Kincaid

asked. "That would have been the best thing."

"There were other cows there. Not just the one," Little Hawk said. "And besides, the young men—and all of our people—are still angry, still very sad over the killing of Young Man Catching Up."

"*Ho!*" The voices spoke again.

"But when the killer is caught, he will stand trial and be hanged," Windy said.

"He will not be hanged," Little Hawk said. "We all know that. For he is a white man."

There was again the loud murmur of agreement from the circle.

"But the cow," Matt said. "The cattlemen must be paid for the cow."

Little Hawk looked impassively at him, and a long moment fell. At length the chief spoke. He spoke without any change in the impassivity of his face. "And who will pay for Young Man Catching Up?"

"A cow is not a man," Quick Thunder said, speaking for the first time, and with anger.

Matt could feel rather than actually see Windy's re-action to the conversation. The scout was seated beside him, and it was instantly clear to both of them that it was no moment to push the matter. Indeed, neither they nor Conway had wanted to bring it up in the first place—but there was Cohoes.

"We want peace with your people, Little Hawk," Matt said. "And you must know how sorry we are about Young Man Catching Up. And you know, too, that we soldiers must do as the law is written."

"As it is written by white men in *Wah-shah-tung*," Quick Thunder said harshly.

Little Hawk held up his hand in restraint, his eyes on the young warrior.

"That is correct," Matt said calmly. "We are soldiers."

"And the law from Above?" said Little Hawk.

"All must obey that one," Windy said. "But underneath that law, you have your laws and we whites have ours."

The Indian chief said nothing. Watching him in the long silence that fell then, Matt felt it was as though the Brulé had simply drawn right inside himself.

After another long moment, Windy said, "There will be cattle coming into the country, cattle belonging to the man who owned the steer that was killed. But they will be kept on federal land, not on the reservation. The soldiers will see to it."

"It is all the land; all the land is one," Little Hawk said. "And what happens even on a small part of the land affects all the rest, affects our people.

"And what of the woolly animals?" the chief went on. "We have had word of them. Now the white man brings them too."

"They are worse than the cows," Wound said, speaking for the first time. "They eat the grass and our horses cannot feed there. We have heard of this. It happened to the Cheyenne."

"The sheep will not come here," Matt said. "The men who guard the sheep will be told."

"But the animals do not know boundaries," said one of the older headmen. "The white man puts up a sign, but the animals cannot understand it."

"*Ho!*" Again the voices sounded around the circle.

"The herders," said Matt, "the men who guard the sheep, and also those who guard the cattle will be told. We will show them on the map, our paper drawing, where they must not let the animals go." He turned his head to look at Windy.

"Little Hawk," said the scout. "There can always be misunderstanding. We must work together. It is hard,

57

but we must." He could feel Quick Thunder watching him as he spoke, could feel the anger coming from him. But he did not turn his head. He went on, "The lieutenant and me know how you feel about Young Man, and we know you don't want any cows or sheep here. That's what the army is for."

"And when the animals do come here, and the white man with them?" Quick Thunder said suddenly. "What must we do? Submit? Never!"

"Never!" Wound echoed.

"Let's cross that one when we get to it," said Windy. He turned to look directly at Little Hawk. "We are your friends, Little Hawk, whether you know it or not."

"That I know, Windy. But it is not you or the lieutenant we do not trust, not you the people fear. It is those others..." And he made a motion with his arm in front of him as if to indicate a wave of the ocean, and then another, and another. "The ones who want to kill us, who never stop coming here. The ones who want to kill our brothers the animals, as they have already killed the buffalo, the brother of the Indian, who once gave us food and clothing and shelter. The ones who do not love the land, and only want to kill it..."

It was late afternoon when Matt and Windy rode back to the patrol.

"Well, old scout, what do you think?"

Windy scratched deep into his neck. "I think we're up to our asses in this."

"Meaning Little Hawk won't keep the peace."

"Meaning Little Hawk *can't*. Matt, the Brulés have already got the army on top of them, now they got cattle, and quicker than soon they'll have the sheep. Little Hawk probably can't hold them young bucks like Quick Thunder. You know those chiefs have to go with what their people want. It ain't like this man's army."

Matt nodded wearily. "I wish to God we'd find something on whoever killed Young Man. But there's nothing. Nothing!"

"Likely a owlhooter or a buff hunter, maybe somebody on the dodge, long gone from the country by now. About as much chance of finding him as a fart in a windstorm."

Windy drew rein as they came in sight of the patrol. For a moment the scout and the army officer sat their mounts, looking at the distant horizon edging the great prairie. Windy slipped one foot out of its stirrup and hooked his leg up over the pommel of his stock saddle.

Reaching up, he began nonchalantly picking his nose. "You know, it only takes one match to start a fire, my friend. Just one."

It was the next morning that the match was struck for the fire. The patrol had camped the night before at Sugar Butte, and they were saddling up after breakfast when Henry Walks Quickly, the Delaware, came pounding into camp.

"Find dead Brulé," he said to Windy Mandalian.

"Where?" The scout was already cinching his roan horse.

Gesturing with his fingers to indicate distance, Walks Quickly said, "Feather Creek."

"Shit." Windy stepped into his saddle.

Within a half-hour the scout and Matt and the Delaware were at Feather Creek, looking down from their horses at the body lying facedown near the gurgling stream of water.

Dismounting, Windy approached the body carefully, looking for sign.

"Shot in the back," he said, bending to the corpse.

59

"Just like Young Man. Maybe our boy ain't left the country after all."

Matt looked at the scattered playing cards lying nearby. "Looks like he died in action," he said wryly.

Windy was squatting, examining some prints in the soft ground. "I'd say somebody caught him cheating, or was a poor loser." He straightened up.

"Two horses," Matt said. "One iron-shod, the other Indian."

"And those are range boots, clear enough."

"An Injun and a white man—and a dead Injun." Windy took off his hat and scratched his head.

"How do you read it, Windy?"

"They were playing cards. Gambling for sure, like the Injuns love to do. I'd say they was playing cooncan, though the game don't matter." He paused. "And he gets shot in the back." He nodded toward the body, which Matt had turned over.

"He's a Brulé for sure."

"And I'd say, seein' the circumstances, that he won, more than likely stripped the man he was playing with and started to ride off. See these prints, and see how his body hit the ground? Made quite an impression."

"You mean he was shot off his horse."

"By the loser, who must of had a hideout gun, for usually the braves play for everything—horses, guns, women if you got any."

"Damn it," said Matt. "How much time do we have before the Brulés learn of it? I mean we're in *trouble*."

Windy had squatted down near a chokecherry bush and was looking at the ground.

"We don't have any time," he said, his eyes still on the ground. "They already know." He pointed at the patch of earth that had been under his scrutiny. "This feller was alone. He was here this morning, coming

60

from"—he looked up and pointed across the creek—"over there, on his way back to camp. They'll be sending a party to bring him in." He nodded toward the dead Brulé. "Better get outta here fast." With his foot in the stirrup, he said, "'Least we know somethin' about this feller now."

"What's that?"

Windy swung up onto the roan. "He's hot for gambling and he packs a hideout. And for some reason he's still hanging around this part of the country."

When they were in their saddles, Matt said, "Windy, you know where the sheepmen are. They'd better move in toward the post. I'll get over to Cohoes. The getaway man can get the news to the Number Nine."

"Good enough."

"Better take a couple of men," Matt said, turning his horse.

"It'll be faster alone."

"I come, Windy," Walks Quickly said.

The scout's lined face spread wide in a mirthless grin. "Better get your red ass movin', then."

six _____

The ambulance rocked along the rutted trail, following the telegraph line over the rolling prairie. Overhead the sky was an azure blue, clean of everything save the hot white sun; and yet it appeared crisp, fresh, as though newly minted. The ambulance seemed to be the only movement, a speck in the middle of the great tawny sea of grass. Bouncing along on steel springs, the battered-looking conveyance did not carry any wounded, but only two civilian passengers, along with the army driver and a single armed escort.

The driver, a spindly individual in faded blue uniform, kept the horses at a sharp pace and apparently was not making the slightest effort to avoid the bumps in the trail for the benefit of his passengers.

The corporal seated beside him, more neat in appearance, was not a permanent part of the equipage. He had been assigned as escort to the two passengers.

Behind the two soldiers sat a man of about fifty and a young woman, along with their luggage, as well as various supplies for Easy Company, including the mail. The couple had come from regimental headquarters and were on the final leg of their journey to Outpost Number Nine.

"We should be there shortly," the man said, after an especially wild lurch of the ambulance almost threw both of them out of their seats. And then, looking toward the back of the two men on the front seat, "How much longer do you reckon, Corporal?"

The escort soldier turned his head slightly in acknowledgement. "I'd say another twenty minutes to half an hour, sir." And he glanced at the driver, who, without taking his eyes off the trail ahead, nodded in agreement, muttering, "Give or take."

The girl, Julie, was just twenty, a slender blonde with flaxen hair, very light blue eyes, small hands, and—as both the soldiers had instantly noted—an excellent figure. Both had also noticed the absence of either a wedding or engagement ring, and so supposed that she and her father, Hawes Thatcher, the U.S. Delegate for the Territory of Wyoming, were visiting Outpost Number Nine on government business.

Hawes Thatcher was a handsome, somewhat stocky man with a tight body, the sort of body that looked as though it had been built carefully out of quality material, and then compressed. It gave the delegate a definite rigidity, which, while helpful in the arena of political life, and possibly even socially, was of little use out on the prairie, where it was essential for survival to remain loose, open to the unexpected, and above all to maintain a sound sense of humor. Hawes Thatcher, it was immediately evident, was a man who took himself seriously. Yet it was just this view of himself that had brought him to decide on a visit to Outpost Number Nine.

"I somehow wish they were expecting us, Father," the girl said, trying to speak softly so that the men up front would not hear.

"What's that, my dear?" Her father had a deep, plangent voice, which was fine for making speeches and ordering people about, but often his daughter cringed as she felt its harsh impact on the social amenities.

"I didn't hear what you said, Julie."

Leaning closer to him, she said it right in his ear.

"But they don't know we're coming only because the

line is down," Thatcher explained. "I suppose some Indians or something."

"They're not sure, sir," the corporal said, half turning toward the back of the ambulance. "But they think it could be the Sioux."

"I thought we were at peace, Corporal."

"Yessir. But you never know with the hostiles. Peace today and they're after your—excuse me, sir—it's war tomorrow."

"I see. Hmm. I see."

They lapsed into silence, concentrating on maintaining their balance in the swaying ambulance. Thatcher turned his head now to look at his daughter, his eyes inadvertently dropping to her waist; and as she caught him looking, she flushed, while he colored slightly high in his cheeks.

"Sorry," he murmured.

"Father, nothing is showing."

"Of course not." He was furious at himself for having been caught looking, and furious with her for speaking on the subject. For though Julie appeared shy in regard to her father's aggressive manners, she had no shyness whatsoever in matters of personal relations, as he had unhappily noticed. She spoke of her condition as though it were something quite usual. Indeed, her attitude embarrassed him; and his embarrassment made him angry.

"They didn't hear anything," she said.

And Hawes Thatcher remained furiously silent, his big jaw jutting out like a rock overhang.

"Father, I do wish you would change your mind. I really don't think this is the way to go about it. I think I should first write—"

Seeing his eyes close, even though he was looking straight ahead, she lapsed into sad, confused silence.

• • •

65

"Ah, it is like the fire." Otio stood on a slight rise of ground with Moro. The man and the dog were looking at the sun rising at the edge of the far horizon. The earth was silent now. Even the birds had stopped singing, as though in acknowledgement of the moment.

"Truly the sun is on fire," Ciriaco said, coming up. "It is not red, but scarlet."

The silence deepened as the shimmering disc rose swiftly above the horizon and entered the great sky, while before it a golden path of light stretched across the prairie. At that very moment, all the birds began to sing.

Otio turned his head away. The light was so dazzling that it blinded his eyes, and he could barely make out the nearest sheep.

It was just at this moment that Quick Thunder and his warriors struck the camp. They came sweeping out of a hidden draw in a racing avalanche of horseflesh, brown skin, and feathers. The warriors were leaning low on their ponies, shooting their rifles from under the animals' necks, with some firing arrows.

Otio dropped to the ground and began firing his Spencer. Behind him, Ciriaco and the others were shooting at will. But the surprise had been deadly. There was no time to count the damage, but sheep had been hit, and a cry of rage told everyone that one of their number was a casualty.

The Indians broke their charge and a second wave of horsemen pounded in, while the first group swung out and disappeared into the hidden draw. It was as though they had vanished from the prairie.

The second wave were crisscrossing in front of the herders, making difficult targets. It was Xerxes who had received a bullet in the arm, and now Michel was hit along the side of his thigh.

Otio, on his belly, was pumping shots at the wave of

Brulé warriors. Ciriaco and the others had spread out wider now, finding whatever cover they could.

From a mile away, Windy Mandalian and Henry Walks Quickly heard the rifle fire. They had been walking their horses, but now stepped quickly into a gallop, checking their rifles as they rode.

At the site of the skirmish, the Brulés had retired into the draw for a moment, and there was no fighting as Windy and the Delaware rode in.

"Xerxes is hit, and Michel," Otio said, running his coat sleeve across his brow. "And six sheep killed. The sons of bitches!"

Windy and the Delaware had swung to the ground.

"They came from nowhere," Ciriaco said. "Like that!" And he swept his two palms together in front of him.

"That's the prairie," Windy told them. "Those draws can hide an army, and when you're at ground level it looks like it's all straight, level ground."

And suddenly the Sioux hit again. They poured out of the draw like a flooding river, their war cries tearing the air, driving right at the herders, who by now had moved in front of the flock of sheep to protect them.

Windy's Sharps added a new note to the fight. Walks Quickly kept up steady fire with his trapdoor Springfield. And again the Sioux broke their charge, not wishing to come too close to those Spencers and Windy Mandalian's highly effective Sharps.

Suddenly a howl went up from one of the sheep dogs as it was hit.

Otio swore. "We must follow the bastards!"

"That's too good a way to get your ass ambushed," Windy warned. "They'll be waiting for you."

"How?"

Windy started to explain, but the language was too difficult for Otio.

67

Ciriaco told it to him in Basque. "They will pretend, Otio. Then they will hide and attack us in the back."

"The bastards!"

Now, suddenly Otio's eye caught a hostile breaking from a stand of cottonwoods.

In one flowing movement he had dropped to his knee, shouldered the Spencer, paused for only a split second, and then squeezed.

The Indian jerked upward in his saddle, and then toppled to the ground.

"Jesus!" said Windy, his jaws racing faster than usual. "That there is neat shootin', if I might say so."

Ciriaco's eyes danced as he looked at Otio. "It sure is," he said, and in superb imitation of Windy, he let fly a wad of spittle at a lump of earth that had been kicked up in the melee.

Windy looked sourly at the sheepherder, but Ciriaco just stood there with a friendly smile on his face.

"Might hire you on as a second scout," Windy said, and he lowered one eyelid slowly, keeping the other wide open. This served to drive Ciriaco into peals of laughter. Otio smiled. It was a good moment, washing away some of the thing that had just happened.

"You got him plumb center," Windy said, nodding toward the fallen Brulé.

Otio nodded. "It was what he deserved," he said simply.

A grin appeared through Windy's whiskers. "And don't tell me that old one about how you was really aiming for the horse."

Ciriaco had to translate, and then Otio took his uncle by the arm and turned him so that Windy could see his back. With his forefinger, Otio felt down Ciriaco's spine.

"Here," he said. "Here is where I aim."

When they walked out to the dead Indian, the herder

knelt down and felt along the brave's spine, as he had done with Ciriaco. "Yes," he said, his finger right on the spot where his bullet had entered. "Right here."

For once, Windy seemed at a loss for words; the only thing to do was to reach for a fresh cut of tobacco.

seven _____

Matt Kincaid rode his bay gelding down a long draw, on the one hand feeling the need to hurry, on the other, wary of the possibility of hostiles. By now a travois or horse would have been sent for the body, but meanwhile the Brulés would surely be painting up. At any rate, he would have to play it that way, for as Windy and he had both noted, Little Hawk would no longer be able to hold back Quick Thunder, Wound, and the others. The big question was whether they could keep Cohoes reined down.

They had reached a buffalo wallow at the bottom of the draw; and beyond that lay a wide expanse of plain, and a small butte. Kincaid called the Delaware scout to him.

"Flying Bird, go see."

The Delaware said nothing, but moved his brown and white pony toward the rear of the patrol, and then kicked it into a trot as he swung off the trail to approach the butte from a different direction.

"Corporal Wojensky, tell the men to stay on the alert."

"Yessir."

Taking out his field glasses, Matt studied the terrain. He saw Flying Bird disappear behind the butte, and presently reappear on the other side, signaling an all-clear.

"Corporal, give the order to move out."

The Easy Company patrol shifted in their McClellan saddles; then, lifting their mounts into a trot, they rode onto the wide plain.

In a moment, Kincaid raised the gait. It was still a good distance to Cohoes's herd of cattle.

The storm had almost stampeded the herd, and Cohoes had moved the cattle close by Fire Creek. The animals were still restive. Here the feed was good, yet there was the feeling of storm still in the air. But Cohoes was impatient to move on. He had only been waiting for the army to appear, having sent word to Outpost Number Nine that he was ready to push on to the Stinking Water.

The boss of the Circle Box brand stood near the chuck-wagon in the early-morning light under a lowering sky. He was listening to the herd, which had started to mill about, the cows bawling here and there. Cohoes held a tin cup of coffee in one hand and a chunk of sourdough bread in the other; he was watching a calf as it darted toward its mother.

"I'd say it was fixing to storm some," said Heavy Bill Haines, the Circle Box Trail boss, clómping up on his high-heeled range boots. "Might move 'em closer to the cutbank yonder." His words came to Cohoes across a saddle rig that was lying on the ground near a pile of dried horse manure.

"Mebbe." Cohoes had squinted at the low sky more than once. "Where is Domino?"

Heavy Bill Haines nodded his head toward some box elders lining part of the creek. "Sawing wood on his back." Heavy Bill, a big man with big hands and feet, made no attempt to hide the disgust he felt about the "foreman" of the Circle Box.

"Guess he needs his beauty sleep," Cohoes said, his face grim; but Elihu Cohoes was not a man to dwell upon unpleasant subjects, and he said no more.

"Riders comin' in," Heavy Bill said, and he scratched himself suddenly, digging deeply into his right buttock.

"I heard 'em."

"Sounds like a bunch."

"Six, I'd put it; no, seven." Cohoes rubbed the side of his long nose with his thumb knuckle, for he was still holding the piece of sourdough. "Might be our army."

He had just emptied his cup and dumped the grounds onto the clump of horse manure by the saddle rig when six mounted infantrymen, headed by Lieutenant Matt Kincaid, briskly rounded a big clump of willow, splashed across the creek, and passed close to the box elders where Ching Domino was sleeping.

"Glad you finally got here," Cohoes said peevishly. "You and your men use some coffee?"

"No time," Matt said. Turning to Wojensky, he said, "Give the order to dismount, Corporal."

"Diss . . . mount!"

"Have them water their horses."

"Water your mounts. Stand ready."

Matt turned back to Cohoes, wondering who the big man standing near him might be. "There's a good likelihood of Indian trouble, Cohoes. You might be getting a visit from a couple of Brulés named Quick Thunder and Wound, along with a few of their friends."

"Injun trouble?" The long, thin cattleman squinted at Kincaid. "What the hell you mean?"

"Somebody shot a Brulé in the back up on Feather Creek not too many hours ago, and it is just what Little Hawk's men have been waiting for. You know anything about it?"

"Shot? Shit!" And Cohoes's good eye swept to the stand of box elders by the creek. He swung back to Kincaid. "I don't know a damn thing about it. Why should I? I been ready to move the herd up to the Stinking Water. You get my message?"

Matt shook his head, studying the cattleman for sincerity; he had noticed Cohoes's quick look toward the box elders. "It's no time to be moving cattle now. Best thing is to hold them here, and be ready for any trouble."

Cohoes looked at the big man beside him. "What you think, Heavy?"

"Should do as the man says, is how I look at it."

Out of the corner of his eye, Matt saw Ching Domino approaching.

But Domino wasn't looking at Kincaid, nor at Cohoes or the big man. He was staring at something directly behind Matt. Suddenly, Kincaid moved toward Heavy Bill Haines.

"Don't know your name, mister. I'm Lieutenant Matthew Kincaid, U.S. Army, Outpost Number Nine."

"Bill Haines. I'm trail boss here."

It worked. Matt held out his hand; after shaking, he turned around to see where Ching Domino was looking. The foreman was staring at the soldier standing next to Malone. Matt could see no expression at all in Private Golightly's face as he looked back impassively at Ching Domino.

The wind stroked the deep grass, causing it to shimmer under the sparkling morning sun. Matt Kincaid felt the heat moving down from his shoulders, along his back, and onto the backs of his hands.

The four riders plus Flying Bird, riding point, were covering the flat ground fast, on a southeasterly course. Kincaid had left Dobbs and Holzer with the cattlemen, keeping Wojensky, Malone, and Golightly.

The sun was straight up as they reached the other side of the draw and swept down onto flat terrain. When they reached the little creek, Kincaid ordered a halt. "We'll let them breathe a little," he said as he swung out of his McClellan saddle. "And they can water some."

Loosening the cinch on the bay horse, and taking the bit out of its mouth, though leaving the headstall and cheek straps ready for a fast rebridling, he turned to see Malone already doing the same with his mount; but Golightly was easing himself gingerly out of his saddle.

"What's the matter, Private?"

Golightly dropped to the ground and turned to face Kincaid, pain suffusing his reddening face. "Got the piles, sir. That saddle don't help any."

"Sorry to hear that, Golightly. The McClellan is a nutbuster, even when you're healthy."

Malone snickered softly, though in sympathy. "Had me the same once, Golightly. When I was whipping the stage one time over at a place called Sundown in Missouri about ten miles from St. Joe. One time the team run away from me on account of I couldn't sit the box decent-like with the piles. And there I was, trying to rein them buggers down, with my asshole hanging out like a buggy-whip socket. Jesus, it was hell, I mean to tell you."

Billy Golightly grinned at that. "Glad I am not alone in this cold world," he said.

"We'll have a smoke and then we'll make it to the post on the next leg," Kincaid said.

"Yessir," Malone said. "If I might say so, sir, I'll feel a whole lot more comfortable when we're back with the army again."

Matt had walked a few feet away and was studying the surrounding terrain. Windy must surely have reached the Basques, but the big question was how much power Little Hawk carried with the Brulés.

They were on the lower end of a long slope, and Kincaid was looking across the creek, up toward the summit. It looked as though there was no break in the flat terrain, but he knew that could be deceptive; a good number of hostiles could be hidden in a gulch that, because of the angle of vision, would not be visible.

He suddenly found himself watching Golightly move toward his horse and slip the bridle back into its mouth. Then he lifted the left stirrup and loosened the cinch and tightened it. The horse was a big bay gelding with three white feet and a wide white blaze on his forehead.

"Stand still, goddammit," Golightly said sharply. "And cut that shit!"

"You know horses, I see," Kincaid said.

"Yessir." Golightly turned. "I've had some experience with them, sir. A lot of them swell their bellies like that, and then when you step into the stirrup they go slack and you end up on your back."

"Where are you from, Private?" Kincaid was looking at Golightly from across his own McClellan.

"Texas, sir."

"I campaigned down in the Staked Plains," Matt said.

"Yes, sir." Golightly was looking back at him, and Matt felt there was more in that look than just respect, and possibly interest. There was—what?—a guardedness. Kincaid thought of the strange way Ching Domino had looked at him.

"How old are you, Golightly?"

"Twenty-two, sir."

"That's what it says on your records?"

"Yessir."

"You know a good bit about horses. And I've noticed the way you handle your Springfield since we've been on this patrol."

"Well, sir, we all had good training."

"Not that good, Private. I'm sure you had some training in weapons before you enlisted. I mean, back wherever you're from."

Suddenly, Billy Golightly grinned. "Well, sir, my dad, he was kind of a . . . well, a lawman."

"Where was that?"

"In Texas, sir. He is dead now, though."

And there it was, that guarded look again; and he'd sounded like he was lying about his father. As Matt squinted at the sun, he decided he'd have Ben Cohen check with Regiment on Private Golightly.

"Mount up," he snapped, and stepped quickly into his saddle. The bay was refreshed, and Kincaid lifted him into a fast canter as they rode briskly toward the long slope.

When at last they reached Outpost Number Nine, Kincaid found that Conway had ordered Taylor and Second Platoon to prepare to move out.

Stepping down from his tired bay, Matt looked over at Taylor and the men, who were sitting their mounts at attention, their eyes locked straight ahead, not a muscle on their faces moving. It was a good sight, he told himself, and he felt something like pride as he looked at the two rows of blue uniforms.

As he walked over to Taylor, who had not yet mounted, the second lieutenant saluted him.

"Captain Conway got you started fast, then, Mr. Taylor."

"I hope fast enough, sir. Windy Mandalian is back. It seems the Sioux attacked the sheepmen, and he rode up just in time to give a hand."

"You're going to swing around the ranches, are you?"

"Yes, sir. We'll warn everyone, and bring anyone in who feels the need."

"Well. I'll get the report from Captain Conway and Windy," Matt said. "Good luck to you, then."

"Thank you, sir."

Taylor snapped a salute to his superior officer, and Matt Kincaid returned it. It felt good, Matt decided as he turned on his heel and walked quickly across the parade to the orderly room. He had just about reached the door when it opened and Captain Warner Conway and Windy Mandalian stepped out.

eight ─────────────

The Basques had moved the band of sheep farther south, down by Powwow Butte, which was near a crossing of the Greybull. The feed was good there, and the crossing would not be difficult for the sheep if it was decided to follow Windy Mandalian's advice and move in closer to Outpost Number Nine. Ciriaco and some of the men had been all for the move, and right away. But Otio was not so sure now, having changed his mind.

"We must hold our independence," he said. "We are not little children who have to depend on the army." He looked at the flashing river as he finished speaking, and then he added, "Besides, we can catch some good trout here."

"But Otio, there is the safety of the sheep." There was urgency in his uncle's words. "You know the *ardiak* always come first. You yourself have said so."

"That is true," Otio said. "And I am thinking of them. But I am thinking we came here to see the conditions. Now maybe we could move up higher into the mountains, rather than down along the plains. We must see."

They were standing in the presence of a beautiful sunset; the almost painful light cast by the dying rays of the sun stretched across the valley and into the willows and box elders along the bank of the singing river.

Yet the herders were watchful. They knew now through grim experience that it was at such times that an attack could come, when—as Otio warned—they were off guard. It was what had happened, and it was what Windy Mandalian had insisted on their knowing.

"That is by God just the moment when them cusses comes at ya!" Ciriaco said, suddenly shifting into his imitation of the scout.

Otio laughed aloud. And Xerxes, coming up to where the two were standing, joined in. But he had to stop, for laughing hurt his wounded arm.

But Ciriaco wasn't through—not at all, he had only just started, spurred now by Julio and Marc, who had come up after looking at the water along the bank of the river.

"I mind the time this feller I knew name of Dutch Charley got plugged in the wrist by his best friend Dutch Fritz." And Ciriaco even lowered one eyelid just as Windy had done, the night he stayed with them after the fight with Quick Thunder and his warriors. "Old Dutch Charley's got his ass in a uproar on account of Dutch Fritz had stole his bed. Well . . ." And here Ciriaco spat out a river of phlegm and spittle. "Well, sir, the doc come and dressed the wound. But after the doc left, Dutch Charley pulled off the bandage and did his own doctorin', pouring kerosene into the wound. Gangrene set in right quick and the next thing anyone knowed, poor Dutch up and cashed in." More spitting. "He is planted over yonder, by Gooseberry Gulch."

His listeners rocked with laughter, slapping their thighs, pounding each other on the back.

"What is the point of your story, Mr. Scout, sir?" Otio asked, picking up on Ciriaco's game.

"Hain't no point. Just tellin' you the dumb things humans sometimes do to theirselves. See, Dutch Charley thought he knowed it all. 'Course he didn't."

"You say we Basques do not know this country, nor the Indian men who will come fight us. And so you want us to go to the soldiers and ask them to fight for us?"

Ciriaco lowered one eyelid, held it for a moment, then raised it.

"I am sayin' it don't hurt to know everything, mister."

Otio laughed. He looked at the others, spreading his hands and shrugging. What, after all, could you do with someone like Uncle Ciriaco?

Ciriaco squatted, his elbows on his knees. He grinned. Suddenly springing upright, he stood stiff and tall, his lips in a straight line, staring straight in front of him. He snapped off a perfect salute. "I, sir, am Lieutenant Matthew Kincaid, Mr. Esteban. The United States Army is at your service, sir."

"Ah, the name was not Kincaid," said Xerxes. "Windy said it was Con . . . something."

"That was the Captain Conway," Ciriaco said, "and his other officer, Matthew Kincaid. They are at the army fort, where we should go," he added, looking darkly at his nephew.

Otio said nothing. Now Ciriaco quickly took a new posture. His expression was totally impassive; he stood erect, but not military. His eyes pierced the atmosphere in front of him. He turned around himself in a circle, and now stood before Otio, his arms folded across his chest.

"I kill white man. We not let white man take our land. we kill, we cut off all his balls!"

They were just about to collapse into laughter again when Little Marc came racing up.

"Indians!" he cried, pointing to the river crossing. "On the other side. On horses!"

Otio snatched up his rifle, which he had leaned carefully against one of the hide panniers in which they carried supplies.

Swiftly he gave orders to the men and the dogs to bunch the sheep closer and tighter, and with Ciriaco and

81

Michel he ran down to a stand of willows at the river crossing, from where Marc had seen the Indians.

"But there are only two," Ciriaco said.

"They are still Indians," Little Marc said.

"There could be more." Otio looked up toward the top of the willows. "Be careful. There is a jay up there, and we do not want him to fly away."

They were silent while the two riders approached on the other side of the river.

"They do not see us," Ciriaco whispered.

"It is true."

"Nor do they look like warriors."

"Maybe they are just going somewhere, not looking for us."

"And maybe they are part of a big party."

"They will see the sheep."

"We will simply have to wait," Otio said with finality.

The two riders, both on pinto ponies, were very close now, almost at the opposite bank of the river. It was clear that in only a moment or so they would be crossing the river and would pass right where the men were.

"I do not think they were in the fighting with us," Otio said. "There is not the paint on their faces." His finger was on the trigger of the Spencer.

"They are well in the range," Ciriaco said.

Otio grunted. He knew that. Yet something kept him from shooting.

"One of them is a woman," Ciriaco said.

"That I have seen," Otio said.

"They will surely see us."

"Yes, surely," said Otio, as the two riders stepped their ponies into the river crossing. The water came just to their hocks, and they went slowly.

They had just gained the bank near the willow where Otio, Ciriaco, and Little Marc and Michel waited, when the man who was in the lead saw them. He kicked the pinto, raising his rifle, just as Otio lifted the Spencer and shot him through the neck.

The woman had started to wheel her horse, but seeing the man fall, she dropped from her horse and ran to his side.

"He is dead," Otio said walking up to her.

Suddenly she had drawn a knife and charged him. But he was quicker, stepping to the side and putting out his foot to trip her, while with the heel of his hand he smashed her in the lower back. She tumbled to the ground, the knife flying out of her grasp.

She lay on the ground, doubled in pain, her breath coming in grunts. Otio watched her while the others kept their distance, no one trusting.

"Two of you watch their backtrail," Otio said, not taking his eyes off her. "And Marc, pull the dead one into the clump of willows."

He let himself relax just a little then, when all at once the fallen Indian woman uncoiled and dove at his legs. But Otio did not fall. Seizing her arm, he swung it around behind her back. A cry broke from his adversary as he pushed her down on her face, with his knee in the middle of her back. After a moment she stopped struggling. Slowly, Otio lessened the pressure on her arm and quickly turned her over on her back.

She was not a woman. She was a young girl. A beautiful young girl.

nine —————————

Before a territory is voted the status of a state, it has one Congressional representative—a delegate. Under the rules of Congress, delegates cannot vote, but Warner Conway, well aware of governmental structure, knew that a delegate such as Hawes Thatcher swung a powerful club in the corridors of the Nation's Capital. The country's ten territorial delegates worked in fairly close accord, for their problems were usually similar; and since the territories covered about half the geographical area of the nation, they wielded an effective power. Maybe a man of Hawes Thatcher's status had no vote, but he did very much have the ear of Congress.

While the captain and Matt were relieved to learn that Thatcher's visit was not official, they were both well aware that for a politician, nothing is really unofficial, and that Thatcher and his daughter had not just dropped in on Outpost Number Nine for a spring vacation.

As Conway put it to his adjutant, "He's not here officially, Matt, on an inspection tour or anything like that—so he says—but he's not here for nothing, and so we're going to have to play with whatever he's dealing."

All of which was in both officers' minds as they sat with the delegate and his daughter, eating supper in the commanding officer's quarters.

Conway watched Hawes Thatcher bowing his head to Flora Conway, his hostess, in acceptance of sugar in his cup of coffee. Reaching into the pocket of his gray broadcloth coat, the delegate from Wyoming drew forth his pipe. "May I?" he started to ask, arching his expression toward Flora.

"But of course, Mr. Thatcher."

"Ah, but won't you try an excellent Havana, sir?" asked Warner Conway, picking up the box on the table beside him. "I pride myself on the quality of these."

Matt watched the pleased smile spreading across Conway's face as he spoke; the captain really loved good cigars.

"Indeed, yes!" Thatcher's eyes lighted up as he returned his pipe to his pocket.

"I have them sent out from Rubin's in San Francisco."

"Do you?" Thatcher rolled the cigar in his fingers, then held it under his wide nostrils. "Ah . . . nothing like a good cigar, is there, Captain? Yes, I know Rubin's." And he bit the little bullet of tobacco out of the end.

"Matt?" Conway held the box for his adjutant.

"Thank you, sir."

"A delicious dinner, Mrs. Conway." Hawes Thatcher's urbane voice fell comfortably into Flora Conway's parlor.

"I'm so glad to see you so pleased, Mr. Thatcher." Flora Conway was radiant, Kincaid thought, watching her as she tilted her head toward Julie Thatcher.

"More coffee, my dear?"

"Oh, no thank you, Mrs. Conway."

Thatcher had lighted his cigar, and now he stretched his long legs out in front of him, crossing one ankle over the other, his eyes following the little cloud of tobacco smoke as it rose gently to the ceiling.

Warner Conway glanced at Julie Thatcher. "Well, Miss Thatcher, I do hope you will find Outpost Nine not too boring."

He felt the warmth of the girl as she smiled at him while accepting an after-dinner chocolate from Flora.

"I'm actually very excited, Captain Conway. I've never been in this part of the country. I was telling Daddy all the way here how beautiful it all is."

"It is beautiful," Flora agreed. "It took me a while to get used to it, I must admit—the size, the silence compared to back East—but..." She spread her hands open on her lap, smiling. "Now I love it."

"Well, again," Thatcher said, "our apologies for just dropping in without warning."

Conway shrugged, with a gentle laugh accompanying his words. "After all, when the telegraph is down, the telegraph is down."

Matt suddenly found Julie Thatcher's eyes on him.

"This is the first time I've ever visited an army fort, Lieutenant," she said, and dropped her eyes to the chocolate she was about to bite into. "Are there many soldiers?"

He thought he detected color in her face, and found himself wondering if Thatcher had noticed.

"There are quite a few. Only this happens not to be a fort, Miss Thatcher."

"Not a fort?" Her blue eyes opened wide in surprise, while her head turned, her lips parting slightly; and Matt felt his pulse quicken.

"It's an outpost," said her father, coming in. "Right, Lieutenant? Regiments have forts, but companies don't. Isn't that correct?"

"That's it," Conway said.

"And the regiment is where we took the ambulance?" asked Julie.

"Yes, ma'am," said Matt. "We look like a fort; it's just a technicality. But the army seems to like technicalities," he added with a grin, and Conway shot him a warning glance.

"And thank heaven they do," he added, bringing his

87

grin to a laugh. "It's the one thing that's structured out here—the army."

Conway, watching the smile on the delegate's face, relaxed. You just could never trust politicians, he told himself. A man like Thatcher could so easily twist Matt's remark into a criticism of the army, and God knows what else. And of course report it in Washington.

"Well, you do appear to be extremely comfortable here, Captain," Thatcher said, his glance covering the room. "Mrs. Conway, I see you're a born homemaker."

"And you, Mr. Thatcher, are a born guest."

Matt and Warner Conway both watched the delegate melt under the superb handling of the captain's lady.

Thatcher drew his long legs in, and now crossed one thigh over the other, taking a drag on his cigar. "I'd say things look good and easy at Easy Company." He chuckled at his own joke.

"Oh." Julie sat straight up in her chair, like a little girl, clapping her hands together. "Lieutenant Kincaid, I have a big question."

Without even realizing it, Matt offered her his most engaging grin. "What is it you wish to know, Miss Thatcher?"

"Why do you call it Easy Company? What a funny name, if you don't mind my saying so."

Everyone had a good chuckle at that.

"There's an Easy Company in every regiment, Miss Thatcher," Matt told her. "The companies go A, B, C, D, E, F, and so on; but the army calls them Able, Baker, Charlie, Dog, Easy, Fox, etcetera."

"What a charming solution to the dullness of simple alphabet letters!"

Matt saw Flora glance at her husband now at a slight pause in the conversation. "If you will all excuse me,

I'll just clear things away," she said, rising gracefully to her feet.

"Please let me help you, Mrs. Conway," Julie said, getting up.

"That would be nice," Flora said. "We'll just take everything out and stack it, so the men can attend to their cigars."

"I love cigars," Julie said, with a smile at her father.

Thatcher frowned severely at her, and she pouted and, picking up the unused silverware, followed Flora out of the room, the conversation toppling into a crashing silence.

"My daughter—uh—has a devilish sense of humor at times," Thatcher said after a long moment. "She delights in trying to get my goat."

"Ah," Conway laughed agreeably, eager to cover the gingery moment. "The ladies certainly know how to do that, don't they?"

In the other room with Flora, Julie Thatcher was controlling an attack of the giggles. "I'm sorry, Mrs. Conway. But you know, Daddy is so terribly pompous at times. And the truth is, I really wanted to say something quite different, and he knew it and that's why he was the way he was."

"He knew what you really wanted to say, dear?"

Julie nodded. "He knew what I really wanted was to *smoke* a cigar. I love them."

Flora didn't miss a beat. "That's nice, dear. Well, you know men mostly don't approve of ladies smoking cigars. I personally don't care one way or the other, so I don't mind if you want to light up."

Julie's eyes opened wide, and she stared openmouthed at her hostess. "Mrs. Conway! I like you. You're a real lady!"

Bugler Reb McBride was in form. His lips, recovered from the sporting encounter at the Silver Tip Saloon, had returned to normal. They were no longer bruised, cut, and swollen, and the notes of his bugle on this particular morning called the men to reveille and not to furious cursing. Reb was again a real bugler. Even Ben Cohen had a smile just barely on his face as he stepped out of the orderly room for morning muster.

Seeing the delegate from the Wyoming Territory standing in conversation with Lieutenant Kincaid, the first sergeant's smile turned to a scowl. When the company orderly, Four Eyes Bradshaw, approached him, Cohen was in no mood for the little corporal's salutation.

"It ain't a nice day, Corporal Bradshaw, it's a shitty day." And Ben Cohen glared up at the clean blue, cloudless morning sky into which the sun had just started to rise.

"Sarge, if I could just quick-like tell you my idea . . ." Bradshaw was a slender young man, nervous, eager, but Cohen knew he had a tough backbone underneath. And he was loyal all the way to his sergeant. But he was at the same time no fawning boot-polisher.

"What bright idea, Corporal? It better be good to offset the way this day is starting." And he glared in the direction of the delegate, for Cohen feared, and with reason, the presence of any meddling government personnel.

"I was thinking of Mr. whatever-his-name-is, I can't remember—the delegate," said Four Eyes.

"Shit."

"No shit, Sarge. Maybe if we handle it right, I got a good idea of how we can get us all promoted."

"Yeah? How?" Sergeant Cohen turned his big head

and looked down at the man beside him. "Hurry it up, we got muster in a minute."

"I'm overdue a stripe, Sarge. Right?"

Cohen didn't answer.

"And you're long overdue promotion with full pay. And if I may say so, the captain and Lieutenant Kincaid are over age in grade, and..." Four Eyes paused to gulp air.

"And what?" The growl came like a little roll of thunder.

"And maybe we can work it with this delegate person to put in a good word."

"Christ!"

"I mean, Sarge, instead of fighting him like we do those damn inspectors, those IG characters, let's pretend to cooperate with him, and maybe he'll help us. What do you think?"

"I think it's time you got your ass into formation or you'll go down AWOL from morning muster!"

"You'll have to excuse my ignorance, Captain Conway, about army matters. It's true I'm the Wyoming delegate in Washington, and the territory is very much army, but I am unfortunately not as familiar with military setup as I would wish to be."

"That's easily arranged, Mr. Thatcher. And look, sir, it's not so easy to remember all the companies and regiments and battalions and what they're made up of. But Matt and I will be glad to give you a good filling-in."

They had just finished breakfast and had returned to the parade. It was, Conway noted, a lovely morning— sharp, yet already starting toward the soft warmth that was characteristic of early spring on the High Plains.

"I see there are a number of Indians about, Captain,

and I must assume they're not hostiles."

"They're friendlies, sir, transients. They stay over at Tipi Town, where you see those tents. And..." A little smile touched the captain's lips. "I must tell you, Tipi Town is a hive of gossip. Sometimes our scout, Windy Mandalian, picks up some useful tips."

It took them a while to cover the post, the captain indicating various points of interest, the delegate asking questions. They were, Conway was pleased to note, intelligent questions, the kind a person who was truly interested in his surroundings would ask, rather than the kind an inspecting officer from Regiment would be digging with, trying to catch someone out. But Conway still felt that Hawes Thatcher had something on his mind.

It was toward the end of the morning when they finally returned to the orderly room. As they entered, Sergeant Ben Cohen looked up from his desk.

"Any action, Sergeant?" the captain asked.

"Nothing, sir."

When they walked into Conway's office, Thatcher said, "I know you're a very busy man, Captain Conway, but I wonder if you could spare me a moment."

"Of course." Conway indicated a chair and sat down himself. "A cigar?"

A rather sour smile appeared on the delegate's face. "Uh—thank you. Perhaps later."

It must be important, Conway reflected, for he had noted how much Thatcher had enjoyed his cigar on the previous evening.

"It's, uh, rather a delicate matter I wish to discuss with you. And, of course, absolutely confidential."

"Of course."

"I mean, it is personal."

"You have my word, Mr. Thatcher, that I will let the matter, whatever it is, go no further, unless in my position as commanding officer of Outpost Number Nine, it is necessary for the welfare of Easy Company and the military situation."

"But of course. I shall trust your discretion."

Hawes Thatcher rubbed his fingers across his forehead, hard, as though trying to rub something away.

"Perhaps I will take you up on that cigar, Captain."

Smiling, Conway opened the box and offered it, then took one for himself. The moment of silence that followed was broken only by the scratching of the match as they lighted up.

Then, suddenly, as though arriving at an ultimate decision, Thatcher blew out a cloud of smoke and said, "My daughter is pregnant, Conway. That's why we're here."

Warner Conway looked at the man on the other side of his desk. He could see it had cost Thatcher something to say that.

"You will wonder why here, at your particular army post. Well, I have been given to understand that Julie's— uh, the man who is responsible for this state of affairs is supposed to be driving a freight wagon on the loop that includes a haul from Cheyenne to Fort Laramie to Fort McKinney." He paused, drawing on his cigar; then, leaning back, a frown on his face, he looked down toward the toe of his boot. "I am not anxious, as you can surely imagine, to encourage any gossip at either McKinney or Laramie. After much thought, I came to the conclusion that here would be the best place to run into the, uh, gentleman. I understand the freighters often stop over at Outpost Nine."

Conway caught the fire in Thatcher's eyes as he spoke.

"What is the man's name?"

"Harry Venable." Thatcher raised his eyebrows. "At least I suppose it's his right name. Ever hear of him?"

Conway was already shaking his head. "We do get freighters through here, but I don't know the name. The sutler might, however. His name is Skinflint Wilson. You could have a talk with him. He's a civilian, of course." Conway looked at the ash on the end of his cigar, then tapped it carefully into the ashtray on his desk. "Might I ask what you intend to do, once you find this person?"

"Don't worry, Captain. I have no intention of killing the son of a bitch. I simply expect to become his father-in-law."

"And your daughter Julie?"

"She will continue to be my daughter."

At the precise instant that the delegate for Wyoming uttered those words about his daughter, the lady in question was lying in her bed half awake, dreaming of the night before, when she was lying on her back with her legs wrapped around First Lieutenant Matthew Kincaid, as they dissolved into an exquisite climax.

She could still feel his marvelous body lying on top of her, perspiring slightly, his hands caressing her rigid nipples, while her own fingers continued to squeeze his balls, emptying them totally.

They had arrived at this happy juncture in their lives following a late-evening promenade about the post. Matt Kincaid had been dutifully following his commanding officer's orders—good soldier that he was—to show Miss Thatcher the salient features of Outpost Number Nine.

As the moon had risen, it seemed only to be expected that their thoughts would turn to matters other than the military, and forthwith the dutiful soldier, eager to follow his CO's orders to the very letter, had whisked the lady into his bachelor quarters where, without the slightest hesitation, she had stripped off her clothes.

Following their initial consummation, they had lain on his bed, still locked in their delightful, totally relaxed embrace. Idly he had started to run his fingers along her belly, then moving up tantalizingly to her firm, full breasts, stroking each nipple in turn, and now bending down to bite them gently into a fantastic rigidity.

"If you keep that up, Lieutenant, you'll have to pay the consequences," she had whispered into his ear.

"My pleasure, Miss Thatcher," he had replied. What a gentleman!

His shaft had stiffened as she continued to play with his balls, and now he was again rigid inside her.

She reached her fingers around its base and said, "I want him in my mouth this time."

"Glad to oblige," he said, withdrawing from her. And then she had slipped down and was licking him, running her tongue around the sensitive head of his erection. Meanwhile, he had plunged his middle finger into her as far as it would go, wiggling it, driving her into a marvelous undulation.

Now she began to suck in long, soaking strokes, as her fist also pumped him. Her sucking grew faster as her fingers returned to his balls. She had just about brought him to his climax when she slowed and, releasing him, gasped, "Please, from behind this time."

And he was on her, driving into her from the rear, her buttocks high in the air as he rode her across the bed, and then they were on the floor.

Now, reliving the delicious scene as she lay in her own bed, Julie Thatcher put her hand down between her legs, and wished fervently that Matt Kincaid was there with her.

Meanwhile, in Captain Conway's office, Hawes Thatcher was relighting his cigar. "I'd better be getting along, Captain, and let you go. Julie's probably getting up by now. She slept late. We're both still a little travel-weary."

ten _____

In the Brulé Indian camp there was no laughter; no young boys threw mud balls with the yellow sticks; there was no war game of Throwing Them Off Their Horses. In Little Hawk's lodge the chief sat with three young warriors. He had filled the traditional pipe and they had smoked silently and watched each other with eyes that were absolutely without any emotion.

Finally, Little Hawk emptied the pipe and cleaned it and put it into its special deerskin pouch.

"Why have you come, Quick Thunder?" he asked, looking at the young man seated opposite him.

"It is to ask your help, Grandfather. You have taught us many things, ever since we were small children. Now we come asking for you to help us." Quick Thunder looked at Wound and at He-in-His-Lodge, sitting to his right and left. "We have fought with the whites, the men of the sheep, and we will fight them again. But there are also the men of the cows, and the soldiers and the soldier fort."

"That I know." Little Hawk spoke softly but decisively, and still with no expression on his lined face. "I have heard of the fighting with the sheep people."

"We ask you to come fight with us, you and the older ones; we ask your help to drive out the whites." It was Wound speaking now, a tall, thin warrior with a scar running from his left eye down to the point of his jaw.

"We have already spoken against this," Little Hawk said. "Yet you went. We spoke of there being too many

97

whites—more of them than there are blades of grass on the prairie. We spoke of the uselessness of fighting them. You did not listen. It has always been a trouble with you. But now you are men. You must think of the people."

"But, Grandfather, they will kill us all anyway, whether we fight or not," Quick Thunder said.

The chief was silent for a long time. He could not argue. What the young men said was true. In his heart he was not in disagreement with them.

At last he spoke. "It is important to survive, that our people may live. We are prisoners on the white man's island. Yes. It is so. But that is for now. If we fight the *Wasichus,* we will all be killed. That does not matter. But if we are all killed, who then will remember our dead? Who will live our way of life? No. We must live. We must survive the white man. We must find our hearts again."

He sat immobile, letting the silence fall all around him.

"But we cannot live like this!" Quick Thunder's eyes were flashing. And immediately he was sorry for having spoken, and bowed his head.

After another long silence, Little Hawk spoke. "Will you not wait to talk with the soldier men again?"

"The soldiers always talk—and lie," said He-in-His-Lodge.

"It is so."

"They will take the land, kill all the animals, bring more of the singing wires and the Iron Horse, and they will dig into the earth for the yellow metal." Now it was Wound who spoke angrily.

"Let us smoke once again," Little Hawk said. "There must not be anger between us. You have taken the young warriors with you, leaving only the old ones and the children. But you do not have enough."

"That is why we ask your help, Grandfather."

Little Hawk was silent. They smoked while the sun slipped toward the horizon, its final brilliant light touching the chief's lodge where it met the ground.

Now the light seemed to grow stronger as the day moved toward twilight, and for a moment it was brilliant along the western edge of the lodge.

At length, Little Hawk stood up. "It is as it is." And he stood before the three warriors, tall, erect, regal in every inch of his bearing, a man who had lived many winters.

His eyes fell on Quick Thunder. "I have known you since you were carried by your mother. And you, and you," he said, looking in turn at Wound and He-in-His-Lodge. But mostly you," he said, turning back to Quick Thunder.

He was still standing tall, outside his lodge, when the three young warriors mounted their ponies and rode away.

Later that night the three Brulé warriors sat around another fire. They sat on blankets on the edge of a buffalo wallow, not very far from the sheepmen, not very far from the cattlemen, and within a day's ride of Outpost Number Nine.

"We must waste no more time," He-in-His-Lodge said, referring to their talk with Little Hawk. "Every moment we delay, the whites grow stronger."

"It was necessary," Quick Thunder said.

"But we already knew that Little Hawk would not tie up his horse's tail and come with us. Nor the other old ones who stayed behind."

"They are all old," Wound said. "They are no longer warriors. They are not like us."

"They are our people," Quick Thunder said. "And it needed to be spoken, what we said in the lodge. Yes, I knew how he would answer. But it needed to be spoken. It was the time for that."

The other two did not argue. All three still felt an uneasiness about Little Hawk's refusal, yet they were resolved in their purpose.

"It is right that the people must live," Quick Thunder said. "But they will not live in the good way. They will simply die one by one, for when the heart is gone, there is nothing."

They sat in silence for a while now, looking at the fire, while around them their warriors waited.

Now Quick Thunder spoke in a new voice, a voice that was sure. "It is true that we are not enough to wipe out the whites. In this, Little Hawk is right."

"What are you saying?" Wound stared hard at his cousin.

"I am saying that I have a plan." Quick Thunder was looking steadily into the fire. "Think of it; we are only one band of the Brulés. But think of it now; we are Sioux. And there are other Sioux. There are the Hunkpapas. There are the Oglallas."

"They will help us!" He-in-His-Lodge said.

"With their help we can rub out the whites, and then we will have our land again. Our people will live, and the game will be good." Quick Thunder had spoken the words as though he were seeing them written in the fire.

eleven _____

In the beginning there had been the mountain men and trappers, and then the buffalo hunters and gold-seekers. Now there were the cattlemen. Elihu Cohoes did not consider sheep part of the picture. Sheep, to put it in a word, were shit.

And cattle was Texas. Elihu Cohoes was not the sort of man to think about tradition; he lived it. The land, the cow, the horse. Himself. It had been he himself who had by God carved it out of the Panhandle. He had staked his spread and it had grown. He was one of a unique bunch. He, Elihu Cohoes, was the tradition.

In the fashioning of his life, there wasn't much that Elihu Cohoes had missed. He had fought the Comanche and the Kiowa, the outlaw and lawman both, not to mention rival cattlemen. A lot of people hadn't agreed with his way of handling things, and a few of them were dead. Not that Cohoes was any gunman. In his day he had been fast, accurate and final, but it was the glinting steel of his character that had gotten him where he was: to the top of the cattle outfits down in Texas.

But he was hurting. Like the traditionally staunch Texas cowman, he had always been a loner; tough as whang leather, decisive as Colonel Colt's Law. But the big blizzard, followed by the cattle fever, had cut him off at the pockets; and at sixty-five going on seventy, even a man such as he didn't find it easy to start over. And compromise came to him like vinegar to water.

In bringing his herd of prime longhorns north to Wyoming, he was staking his last card on recouping. This was the big one. And the compromise was Ching Domino—and Larrabee Hogan. But Hogan had been taken by the law and stashed in the pen, and his former partner, Domino, had brought the thousand head—half Hogan's and half his own—to move them north with the Circle Box, the stolen beeves mixing in with Cohoes's brand. It was risky, Cohoes knew, but it was his chance to recoup and put together a stake; and he had never balked at risk. With himself and Heavy Bill Haines ramrodding the drive, and Ching Domino as their protection, he was pretty sure of the outcome. But then, news had come that Hogan had busted out. There could be only one trail he'd be taking.

It was playing it close to the vest, the way he'd always liked it. But the pot had gotten even more gutty when they'd discovered that soldier who looked for sure to be Hogan's kid brother, and in the last place you'd ever expect—right under their feet, right here in the United States Army! Did that mean Hogan would be around? He had raised the kid, Domino told him; they'd been real close. And if the kid had recognized Domino...

"'Course, we don't even know if Hogan knows the kid's here," Cohoes was saying as they squatted near the herd, with a small fire between them. "And if the kid recognized you."

"I don't figure he did. I only seen him a couple of times when he was real small. Hogan sent him out to be raised by an old couple."

Ching Domino belched at the fire. They had moved the herd up toward the north fork of the Greybull, and were holding them now as they considered whether to move in closer to the army at Outpost Nine, or push on up to the Stinking Water. Heavy Bill Haines and a couple of hands had scouted ahead earlier that forenoon and reported Indian sign—a lot of it—and at another place, sheep, though they'd not hung around to actually see the critters.

"The thing is whether Hogan hisself is in the country," Domino went on, his guttural voice heavy in the evening air. "Funny coincidence, them two Injuns backshot, the one with cards in his hand. Hogan was always crazy for the cards."

"You're saying he got up here ahead of us?" Cohoes was eyeing Domino sideways through that one eye that could still see.

"I wouldn't want to get previous with that notion," Domino said. "But it makes sense. Huh—it's what I'd do, if I was in his boots."

Cohoes nodded, looking down between his legs as he squatted. He had picked up a small branch and was drawing aimlessly on the ground. "Reckon I'd do the same."

"So what you figger would be his play?"

"He'll be wanting to kill us, Mr. Domino. What the hell do you think!" Cohoes had not raised his head as he spoke.

A flash of color swept into the other man's face, showing bright against his black hair. "Then what do you think we oughta do, Cohoes? Hell, we can't just sit here waitin' to be shot at."

Now Cohoes looked up. Snapping the stick between his callused thumb and fingers, he said, "Do? The only sensible thing to do is to kill him first." And he stood up.

"But now, for Chrissake? Where is he? He can hide out in this goddamn country forever, and he can just pick us off whenever he wants." Ching Domino had come to his feet, and now, as Cohoes started walking toward the chuckwagon, he fell in with him. "Shit, Cohoes, we're sitting ducks."

Cohoes stopped suddenly and faced his foreman. His voice was harder as he said, "Now you know why I was so hot to get an escort up to the Stinking Water. I had a notion he might of gotten ahead of us."

"But those soldiers we got with us are for fightin' the Indians. They're not gonna stoop for—"

"All cats are gray in the dark," Cohoes cut in. "And anyways, we have got something better," Cohoes said, and his voice was soft now, sinewy, as he peered at Ching Domino.

"What d'you mean?"

"We have got that little soldier boy. Or we will if we can play it right."

"How are you figuring that?"

"We can take him if we have to, and we know that Hogan will have to behave himself."

"But Cohoes, that's the army you're messin' with."

The look that came into the cattleman's eyes now held the other man as though he had a hand gripping him. "Wrong. It's the army *you* are messin' with. It's your baby. Remember? You're the regulator half of this here outfit."

Ching Domino's voice was softer as he said, "And maybe I got to say no to that, Cohoes."

"Mebbe. Mebbe. Only you ain't going to. On account of you're more scared of me than you are of the U.S. Army, Mr. Domino." And without another word, without even a look at Ching Domino, Elihu Cohoes continued on his way to the chuckwagon. He was thinking how much he wanted a cup of coffee.

It was an extraordinary day. The sky was brilliant and without a single cloud. The cleansing of the storm was still apparent in the fresh, crisp air, the lush grama grass that shone brightly green under the dancing sun. It was a day that Matt Kincaid could feel moving right into his body, not stopping at the skin, a day that somehow brought him a fresh mindfulness of himself and his sometimes lonely life, the life he loved. It was extraordinary.

For a while the patrol had ridden in a diamond formation, but now Matt had ordered them into two columns, with himself and Windy at the head. Malone was riding point, and Gillies was getaway man. Billy Golightly had been left back at the post, due to his condition. He had asked especially to come along, but Kincaid hadn't wanted a good man ruined and had refused the request. Now the men were spread well apart so that they would not offer an easy target.

"Should be contacting Taylor pretty directly now," Windy said, spitting over his horse's withers. "Thing is, it appears the cattle and sheep have been moving closer to each other, instead of closer to the post, like they was advised."

"I guess that figures." Matt Kincaid's tone was wry. "You got two men there who don't like to step back one bit." He squinted at the sky, noting the place of the sun, and said, "The sheep are moving down southeasterly from the Absarokas, and the cows are coming north along the Greybull. It'll be a miracle if they don't meet."

"Maybe Taylor's talked some sense into them." Windy gave a throaty, mirthless chuckle. "All we need then is the Sioux in the middle when they lock horns."

"Might arrange that little thing," Matt said with a big grin.

They had left Outpost Number Nine at dawn, leaving Third Platoon under Fletcher to hold things down, along with Captain Conway and Sergeant Ben Cohen.

The plan was for Taylor and Second Platoon to cover the cattle and the sheep, as well as the outlying ranches. His orders were to leave a few men with Cohoes, and there would be the two men already assigned by Kincaid; and men would be assigned the sheepherders. Or, if necessary, the plan could be modified to leave small detachments with any ranches. Kincaid, Windy Mandalian, and First Platoon would now follow up; the Sioux would not expect another platoon of soldiers to come so quickly into the field. Thus, the move could give Easy Company the advantage. And as Matt had pointed out to Conway, they were going to be spread pretty thin, and needed whatever help they could get; especially with the none-too-wholehearted cooperation of the herders and cowboys.

The three men had talked it over in the predawn over scalding coffee. Matt had enjoyed—to put it mildly—his one-night stopover at the post following his visit to the Cohoes herd; seldom had he met such a delightful partner as Julie Thatcher. It had come as a shock when, just as they were leaving Conway's office that morning, the captain had taken him aside and confided Hawes Thatcher's news about his beautiful daughter. But of course, as Windy was wont to comment on such things, "If they're old enough and willing, they're old enough and willing."

This nugget, which Matt remembered from that invaluable lode which he and Conway privately called "Windy's Wisdom," sufficed to soften the rude surprise to his New England upbringing. But Matt could not help reflecting, as he rode now, that those teasing eyes, those eager lips, and that superbly undulating body in the heat of action simply mowed down any concern for anything other than the moment.

Windy had picked up sign of the cattle.

"They're heading toward the Stinking Water, just what they was told not to. 'Course, we can't tell if Taylor's met up with 'em yet; I mean up ahead."

The two columns had reached the bottom of a timber-fringed gulch, and Matt called a halt.

"We'll let the horses blow," he said to Windy, then turned to Sergeant Gus Olsen. "Sergeant, give the order to dismount."

Olsen, a knobby veteran of the Civil War and the Western campaigns, half stood in his stirrups—enjoying immediately the relief to his battered buttocks—and foghorned the order, *"Dis...mount!"*

Kincaid and Windy swung down from their mounts at the same time. Matt took off his campaign hat to relieve the pressure of the sweat band around his head, and then put the hat back on at a slightly different angle. As he loosened the bay's cinch, he was aware of the smell of damp uniforms, saddle soap, plug tobacco, and horses. For even though the day was sharp, the men had ridden hard and they were heated. Now the stinging odor of horse urine spread into the air, and there was the jingling of bridle hardware on the shuffling mounts as they bent to the lush grass.

"Better take a look-see up ahead," Windy said. "I'll send Walks Quickly."

"Good enough." Matt suddenly remembered the cigar Conway had given him—"a present for back-to-back patrol duty"—and he had the impulse to light it, but decided to save it for when they bivouacked.

Windy, in the meantime, was looking around the area for sign. Kincaid watched him. He was always fascinated with the way the scout worked. Windy could read the land, the sky, nature, like a letter from home. And the best thing was that he was always generous in imparting his knowledge to Matt.

"Well, part of the herd come through this way, as you can see for yourself," he told Kincaid now. "What do you say to that?" He kept his eyes on Matt, who was

107

studying the ground by a clump of sage. "See anything else?"

"A horse, coming up behind," Matt said.

"How do the prints look, real fresh or what?"

Matt realized the scout had already seen the tracks. "Fresh, I'd say."

"Meaning?"

"The rider came along sometime after."

"But not too long?" Windy cocked his head, a little smile creeping into his eyes.

"Not too long."

"White man?"

"The horse is shod."

"Something else?"

"Horse is about to throw a shoe." Matt bent closer to the print. "I'd say the left forefoot."

Windy nodded. The smile had moved from his eyes to his mouth and now it broke across his face into a grin. "By God, you're gettin' to be a right smart tracker, Mr. Lieutenant, sir!"

Matt grinned with pleasure, and then laughed at himself, seeing how he was responding like a kid. There was always something about the way Windy Mandalian worked that was irresistible.

The two of them stood near each other, looking down at the horse and cattle tracks, while the sun played on their backs and shoulders.

"Two thousand head is one hell of a lot of beef, Matt."

"It's also money on the hoof. You can see why Cohoes is so damned eager to get them to the railhead at the Stinking Water."

Windy was picking a piece of tobacco out of one of his front teeth with his little fingernail, his whole face contorted with the effort. At last, meeting with success, he said, "You got any notion how come Cohoes has a man like Ching Domino on his payroll? I'd lay odds he's not had a day's work outta that boy in a month of Tuesdays."

"Like you said, Windy, he's got to be a regulator."

"Yes indeedy. Look at them tracks again." The scout squatted, and Matt followed suit. "See here, he ain't a part of the drive," Windy said.

"How the hell do you figure that?"

"You seen how he's about to throw a shoe there."

"Sure, but I don't see how that makes the horse and rider not a part of the cattle drive."

"That's easy enough to figger. If he was one of Cohoes's drovers and his horse was in that condition, he'd of picked another mount out of their cavvy. But since he's still ridin' that same animal with that loose shoe, it's for sure he ain't one of Cohoes's men."

"You're saying he's following the herd."

"Following the herd. Or maybe following Cohoes and Ching Domino."

They were silent for several moments as Windy carved himself a fresh chew of tobacco from his seemingly endless supply. Kincaid decided it was time to move out.

He had just turned in the direction of Sergeant Olsen to give the order when Henry Walks Quickly came pounding up, his pony's hooves drumming on the hard-packed ground.

"Soldiers up ahead. Bad fight with Brulés. Some wounded."

"Lieutenant Taylor, was it?"

The Delaware nodded three times. "Lieutenant and his men. I met point man. Soldiers headed this way."

Kincaid swung on Olsen. "Give the order to mount, Sergeant!"

"Moouunt . . . up!"

To a man the platoon swept into their saddles, and Kincaid gave the signal to move out. In a moment he was bouncing his fist overhead to signal a gallop.

twelve

"But Father, I really don't see the sense in staying here at this army outpost in the *hope* that Harry is going to turn up. I mean, we could be here for months!"

"My dear, I have it on pretty good authority that Venable is driving freight on the route that comes right through here, as I have already told you. He actually delivers freight here to the sutler's store."

"But when? Once a year, every six months?"

"He is due now, according to my information. Any day now. I think we timed it just right."

It was morning and the Thatchers were seated in their quarters in the guest barracks. Dutch Rothausen, the mess sergeant, had sent coffee over at the captain's request, and so they were relaxing after having enjoyed another evening with the Conways.

Hawes Thatcher was enjoying his first cigar of the day, leaning back comfortably in the overstuffed armchair, his legs up on a footstool, his eyes carefully appraising his fingernails.

"No, my dear, the best thing is simply to wait. We won't stay here more than two weeks. I'll wager our Mr. Harry Venable will show up in less than a week. And when he does . . ."

"Father, you promised."

"Yes, Julie, my dear daughter, I promised. And I will keep my promise. I will simply tell that . . . *gentleman* . . . that he will do the right thing by my daughter, or he'll be sorry. Damned sorry!"

Whipped into anger by his own words, he got up and strode into the adjoining room, leaving a trail of cigar smoke in his wake.

Julie continued to sit where she was, with her hands in her lap. She felt quite helpless. After a moment she rose and walked over to the large wall mirror and stood looking at herself. The mirror was big enough for her to see down to her knees, which was all she wanted. She studied herself head-on, then turned, examining one side, now the other. Did it show? No, not yet. She had only missed one period, so things were not all that far along. But soon it would show. And what then? What if Harry didn't show up? What if he refused to marry her? But no. Nobody refused Hawes Thatcher.

"And meanwhile," Thatcher said, coming back into the room, "I can be looking over the situation here. In my line of work it certainly doesn't hurt to have some grassroots information on things like the army and the frontier."

His good humor restored—he had whipped down a neat shot of brandy in the other room—Hawes Thatcher put his hand on his daughter's shoulder and looked her steadily in the eyes.

"I only hope that you will bear a son, my dear."

Julie colored slightly, and her eyes seemed to grow wider. "And what if I don't, Father?"

"What if you don't what?"

"What if it's a girl?"

He studied her a moment, noting her seriousness. A slow smile appeared at his eyes and mouth. "Then of course I'll forgive you, my dear." And he dropped his hand from her shoulder.

Hawes Thatcher was a politician all the way through, which meant that since his chief purpose in life was to perpetuate himself in office, he had limited intelligence.

He did not notice the pain that filled his daughter—the dullness that swept into her eyes, the tension that entered her young body, as he said those words. But of course he had been manifesting such behavior toward her all her life, even though he loved her. For after all, as he had told Warner Conway, she was his daughter.

It was the next day that it finally got to young Julie; and over a cup of tea she told the whole story to Flora Conway. After which she wept in the older woman's arms, had another cup of tea and a shot of brandy, and discovered that she had a friend.

Flora always took the practical approach. "My dear, the important thing is that you stay well. And when your young man turns up, simply speak openly with him. After all, he's had all this time to think things over, and I'm sure he'll look at the situation in a different light now."

Flora wasn't sure at all, but what else could she say to the unhappy young girl? And she wondered if it might not be a bad idea for Warner to have a word with Thatcher or—maybe better still—with Harry Venable.

"Mrs. Conway—"

"Call me Flora, dear."

"Flora, what I said the other night—remember? I told you that you were a real lady and I liked you."

"I'm glad you like me, Julie. About the lady part, well..." Flora made a face. "I wouldn't want anything like that to get around and ruin my reputation."

"Mrs. Con—I mean, Flora..."

The captain's lady had been moving a book to another place on the side table next to her chair, and she looked up now to find Julie's great, liquid gaze upon her.

"Flora, I...I wish you were my mother."

Flora Conway's mouth opened, and for a moment she didn't know whether to cry or laugh. "Your *mother!*

Couldn't I at least be your *sister?"*

And when Julie realized what she had said, the two of them burst into a great peal of laughter.

Billy Golightly's unfortunate physical condition had virtually disappeared and he was himself again. This good fortune was the result of two factors: rest from torturous contact with the McClellan saddle, and an ointment prescribed, and in fact prepared, by Dutch Rothausen, the mess sergeant and healer-in-residence at Outpost Number Nine. Billy had been so elated at having his rear end restored that he put in extra time in Dutch's kitchen without having either been asked or ordered.

"I always thought there was something the matter with that mysterious kid," Sergeant Ben Cohen said when Rothausen started singing his brag about the new recruit who actually *wanted* to pull KP.

"Jesus!" answered Dutch to the first sergeant's comment, and stomped off in disgust.

Meanwhile, Private Golightly was now pulling stable detail—officially—a job that no one but himself knew he liked. He loved horses. He loved the way they smelled, felt, looked. He had ridden since he was a button down in Texas, and he knew horseflesh like the best of them.

Billy also knew guns, and that was something he also kept to himself. There had been that moment on patrol when Lieutenant Kincaid had spoken to him, noting his ability with his mount, but it hadn't gone any further.

He had learned at an early age from his older brother Larrabee that you never told anybody anything. "Don't trust nobody but yourself, kid—then you'll know who sold you out," was how Larrabee Hogan had put it.

Billy Hogan had loved guns almost as much as horses. And he loved his older brother. Larrabee had raised him

114

from a little kid, their parents having been shot and killed by the vigilantes. The vigilante leader had apologized the next day when it had been discovered that the Hogan couple were the wrong party. Billy often relived that scene. He couldn't have forgotten it, even if he wanted.

"We are sorry, boys, we made a bad mistake. Took your paw and maw for another couple." The vigilante leader had come to the cabin with two other men, who stood silently beside him. All three wore beards, big boots, and guns.

Larrabee Hogan had stood there silently for a long moment. Beside him, his kid brother, age seven, had been more or less successful in fighting his tears, only he couldn't control his body and it had started to shake.

Larrabee was just nineteen, and he had said finally, "A *mistake*, mister? And you are *sorry* for that mistake?"

"We are sure sorry, son. We are all of us sorry for that terrible mistake."

Larrabee had been standing on one side of the big sofa, with the back of it facing the three men, and behind them the door of the cabin.

"Well," he'd said, "then maybe you can also be sorry for your second mistake—telling me." And he had reached down and grabbed the cutdown shotgun lying on the sofa cushions out of sight of he visitors, and with that wide scatter had cut those three vigilantes just about in two.

In the stable at Easy Company, Billy felt the sweat damp on his forehead as, forking out the manure, he relived the scene, as he had done many times; the bodies lying like scarlet pulp on the floor, then the two of them running to their horses and racing away. And it always made him sweat. But it also made him feel good.

There had been the years on the trail, the outlawing that Larrabee took to like a snake to its skin. Larrabee had taught him everything—horses, guns, men; he had taken the boy everywhere with him. Finally he had left him with an old couple down in Nogales. Billy hadn't wanted it, but Larrabee had insisted, the law being so close on his trail. Billy had hated it at first, missing his brother badly, and some of the men he rode with. But he got used to the old couple, the Hardies, who ran a few head of cattle outside Nogales; and he even learned to read and write.

When news came that Larrabee Hogan had been taken by the law, the Hardies, who were having hard times keeping bread on the table, said why didn't he join the army. Billy asked for the cavalry, and ended up in the mounted infantry, which was just as good, and maybe better.

It was late in the day when the stable detail was dismissed. Young Billy was walking alone across the parade when he saw the girl. She was obviously looking around for some kind of directions.

"Can I help you, Miss?"

"I was looking for the paddock and the horses," Julie Thatcher said.

Billy Golightly looked into those deep blue eyes and said, "I'd be proud to show you, Miss."

thirteen_____

The girl had eaten nothing. Although she had also refused water when it was offered, Otio had seen her take some from the canteen when she thought no one was looking. Nor had he or any of the others been able to get her to speak. Not a word. She just stared at them impassively, not even showing grief for her dead companion.

The Basques had finally decided that the young warrior was neither her husband nor a relative, but probably an escort, since they seemed to have been simply traveling from one place to another.

"I am sure it was that," Otio said as they discussed it. "He was young. He was probably a warrior, but I do not believe that they were related, for she does not show that much sorrow."

"And surely they were not hunting," said Little Marc.

"No—traveling."

"He was a handsome young man. Yes, a warrior."

"And she," Ciriaco noted, looking at his nephew, "is beautiful."

"She is an Indian," Xerxes said gruffly, catching something in Ciriaco's tone of voice.

Ciriaco threw his hands out in an elaborate shrug. "So—she is a beautiful Indian."

Indeed, Otio Esteban was in full agreement. He found it difficult to keep his eyes away from her. She, for her part, was completely aloof, refusing every effort at contact from the sheepherders. She lay or sat on the blankets with her legs and hands tied only when the guard might absent himself; otherwise she was not bound.

"A princess in captivity," Ciriaco observed.

Otio spoke to her. "We keep you captive only so you will not tell the other Indians to come and fight us because of the young man."

The girl said nothing. Did she understand English? They tried Basque on her, but there had been no response.

"The young warrior raised his rifle," Otio explained. "He would have killed me. If I had not shot him, I would be dead." Otio had never been given to explaining things, but in the present situation he felt the need. But he only said it once.

When they moved camp, the girl had to be tied onto one of the mules, for she refused to walk. Indeed, it was soon apparent that she had injured her leg or foot.

"She might be pretending not to speak the language," Ciriaco pointed out, "that is, the English." He made a face. "No one can be expected to understand the Basque."

"She could pretend the bad leg too."

"For certain."

"They are clever, the redskins."

Now they had reached their new campsite, high up, overlooking a great expanse of plain that ended at a large stand of timber on a rise at the horizon. Otio had told them that he wanted to look at the feed on the other side of the timber, for it was not good where they were.

"How long will we keep the girl?" Xerxes asked.

"Until we have decided what we will do."

"But how? Should we not give her to the soldiers?"

"I do not know," Otio said, and they could see that he didn't want to talk about it. "Tomorrow," he said, "we must go farther south and east, over there." He pointed toward the timber.

That night she accepted both food and water. It

118

seemed that it had been during the struggle with Otio after her companion had been shot that she had been hurt, for no one remembered seeing her limp before that moment. Still, she would allow no one to examine her foot or leg, whichever it was. And so, when finally she got up and walked about the tent, it was with a limp.

That evening, Otio tried again to get her to talk, but finally had to give up. He had been sitting crosslegged, facing her, and at last he got to his feet and went to the back of the tent to rummage in a pile of robes and blankets.

For the first time since her capture the girl showed some expression on her face when she saw the guitar. Otio pretended not to notice her guarded interest as he seated himself again, crossing his legs, and began tuning the shiny instrument.

"Aah!" Ciriaco exclaimed, entering the tent.

Otio began to strum, searching himself for a song. He started to hum. It was a song of the mountains, of the lush green Pyrenees of *Euzkadi*, the country of the Basques. With flowing ease his deep voice formed words in his native tongue. In a moment Ciriaco joined him. Now, through the tent opening came Michel and Little Marc and Old Enrique with the twisted foot from the day he was born. The tent was suddenly full of men singing, clapping, or just listening.

The song over, Otio stopped as gently as he had begun, and the group sat in silence finally broken by the choppy bark of a coyote.

Two of the men started to their feet.

"The *coyotl* sounds from the *barrankua* up ahead, the canyon," said Xerxes. "But we will see."

"Take Pinto," Otio said, and the dog, who thought he had slipped inside the tent unnoticed, rose with his tail wagging.

119

"Sing more, Otio." Ciriaco looked at the girl. "He, Otio, is our true *bertsulari,* our troubadour," he said, speaking directly to her.

Otio's fingers had already started to stroke another song. "Julio," he sang, "Julio, bring, oh bring the *xah-akua!* And we will drink and sing and be wise with wonderful wine!"

Everyone clapped their hands and laughed.

The sheepmen joined now in the songs, some of which Otio made up on the spot, others they had known since their childhood. And they drank the wine—but not too much, for there were the sheep, and Otio would not allow them to forget what they were there for.

He had doubled the guard, and sent out all the dogs. He tried not to look at the girl, though he could now and again feel her eyes on them as they sang. One or two of the older men even tried a few dance steps in the cramped space, to the laughter of their companions.

Otio played as he had never played before. It was good. It was really a good moment. And he knew that he was playing and singing not only to the sheep and the sun and the moon and the sky, to the whole of life. He was singing to the girl, the girl with the deep dark brown eyes and the raven-black hair hanging along her breasts in two long braids, and to her brown skin, soft and mysterious as dusk.

He stopped playing, his fingers just reaching the end of his song, the sound melting into the silence that now took over the tent.

He looked at the shawl the girl wore around her shoulders. "I will call you Yellow Shawl," he said.

She said nothing, yet he felt a change in her. Then Ciriaco came back into the tent; he had been looking after the sheep.

"I will take a walk," Otio said, putting down the

guitar. He wanted to stay near the girl, but the sheep must come first, always the sheep must be first. When he returned in a little while, the herders were telling stories.

Then Ciriaco took over. He imitated the soldiers, the Indians, and Otio. In outrageous pantomine he asked the girl if she was married, if she had a man. He was remarkable and indeed graphic, and always funny. The herders rocked with laughter. And finally—none of them could believe it—a smile stole into the eyes of their captive, who instantly looked down to hide it.

With her eyes down, she spoke. "My husband is gone."

"She speaks!"

"She speaks English language!"

Ciriaco leaned toward her. "It was him, your husband? The one killed?"

"No. Twelve moons gone from the time there was the fighting at Big Rock with the Crows."

Otio had been wiping his guitar with a piece of cloth. Suddenly he raised his head and found the girl looking at him.

"I am Morning Flower," she said.

fourteen

Second Lieutenant Taylor and his men, riding away from the Cohoes herd of cattle, skillfully avoided an Indian ambush at Franc's Crossing, thanks to the alertness of the point rider, Private Myles Moynihan.

Mr. Taylor was a fairly modest man; still he felt pretty puffed up from having outfoxed the Sioux. There were indeed moments when Taylor, like many a young officer out of West Point, chafed under the tough yet resilient discipline of Easy Company's adjutant, Matt Kincaid. Taylor sometimes had difficulty figuring out Kincaid's motives. Sometimes the man was as strict as a whip, while on other occasions he simply seemed to go along much too easily. In short, his superior officer did not manifest the inflexibility of "the book," which Taylor and so many graduates from the Point honored often at the expense of common sense.

Still, there was no question that Mr. Taylor admired Matt Kincaid, and sought to impress him—not as a fawning seeker of favor, but to satisfy the need for approval from someone who was so clearly his superior. Thus, the cute outmaneuvering at Franc's Crossing was a coup; and Taylor chuckled to himself at the choice of the word.

The patrol rode briskly across the meadow that separated Franc's Crossing from a line of young cottonwoods, through which the trail led west and north, rising to the higher ground where Taylor expected to encounter the Basque herders later that day.

It was a day in which the clarity of the blue sky rang

with a stillness penetrated suddenly by a flock of wild geese, whose disciplined flight emphasized the vast emptiness. Lieutenant Taylor sighed as they approached the cottonwoods, the trail disappearing into the dark interior.

He was mentally writing up a dashing report for Kincaid and Captain Conway, when suddenly an appalling avalanche of screaming warriors swept out of the trees, while another row of horsebackers poured out of a gulch just off to the right, catching the patrol in a neat pincer. To his dismay, Taylor realized he had been completely fooled by the fake ambush at the Crossing.

Taylor did not lose his head. He had seasoned men in his command who, following his orders, dismounted and found cover, horseholders dropping back with the mounts, ready to bring them forward as needed.

The men on the ground instantly began returning a solid fire at the attackers, who seemed to be coming from all directions, though Taylor realized that in fact they were not surrounding them, thus running the risk of shooting one another across a circle, but had executed a more deadly attack in the form of an L.

The first waves left two men wounded, and Moynihan, the point rider who had spotted the earlier false ambush, dead. The Sioux swept back to the cottonwoods and the gulch, giving the soldiers a moment while Taylor ordered them to keep spread out in a staggered line.

The lieutenant was a brave man, but he suddenly knew a terrifying moment as he waited for the next attack, as a silence fell across the meadow. The silence lasted barely a minute, and then the Sioux came pounding in, firing rifles and arrows, sweeping into the lines of the prone soldiers, swinging war clubs and axes.

And again they were gone.

Only this time there was no silence. All at once the sharp coughing of a bugle broke over the meadow, and

Taylor, stunned with disbelief, saw the blue soldiers pouring in from his flank. By the time Kincaid and his men reached the beleaguered patrol, the hostiles had vanished.

"In the very nick of time, sir, and thank God," Taylor said ruefully after saluting Matt and nodding a greeting to Windy Mandalian.

"Sometimes it happens like that," Matt said.

Taylor seemed to take a fresh hold on himself. "But aren't you going after them, sir?"

"I haven't lost my sanity yet, Mr. Taylor."

Taylor could have chewed his tongue right out of his mouth as he felt his face flaming with embarrassment. "God, sir! Will I ever learn!"

"In this country, Mr. Taylor, you only get to make one mistake. Windy read your tracks back at Franc's Crossing. That trick they pulled is the oldest in the book."

"And I almost did it again!" Taylor was bleak with despair. He looked so miserable that Windy let a heavy chuckle fall, but said nothing.

Matt was looking at Taylor's shoulder. He had noticed the rather heavy salute the lieutenant had given him.

"You've been hit?"

"Just a crease, sir. Some of the men are hit badly. And Moynihan is dead."

"Better get a casualty count right away." Kincaid turned to Gus Olsen, who was still mounted. "Sergeant, dismount and cover the area." He turned back to Taylor while Olsen barked out the order. "Was it Quick Thunder?"

"I don't know, sir." A wry grin formed itself as he said, "They were quick. And like thunder. They came like lightning."

"And like lightning they took off," said Windy, easing himself into the conversation. "It's got to be Quick Thunder." He held up an arrow. "Sioux arrow. And the fight was Little Hawk's style. Quick Thunder took some good lessons from him."

By now the casualty count was in. "Four men wounded, sir. McGee and Barton aren't bad, but Williams and Ferrandi need attention, shot in the neck and leg. Moynihan's dead, and Furman is gutshot. It don't look like he'll make it, sir."

"How many dead hostiles?"

"The Sioux took whoever was hit with them, sir."

"Of course." Windy stood swing-hipped, his thumbs hooked in his wide leather belt.

"And the cattle?" Matt kept his eyes on the men who were helping the wounded as he spoke to Taylor.

"The cattle are all right, sir. We were on our way to the sheep. Cohoes kept saying he wanted to push on up to the shipping point, and he wanted a full escort. I left two men, and along with Dobbs and Holzer, that makes four. But I advised him to stay where he was."

"And the ranches?"

"The McKinneys and the Cowries are coming in. The rest, up around Grass Creek, want to stick it out. They're pretty close together. I told them I didn't like the idea, but they insisted."

Matt studied the sun for a moment. "You'd better get right on back to Number Nine. You'll have to go slow with your wounded."

"Yes, sir."

Kincaid said, "We will take over the rest of the patrol. I think we'll check back on Cohoes just in case Quick Thunder decided on a visit."

Windy looked across at Matt carefully. "You suspicion something besides Quick Thunder?"

"Just as you do. We might check out those tracks.

126

Our friend might decide to make his play."

"Sir . . ."

"Yes, Mr. Taylor."

"Sir, request to stay in the field. I can send a detail back with the wounded."

"Lieutenant, I am not sending you back because of your stupidity in riding into an ambush so easily, but because I want you back at the post."

"Yes, sir." Taylor appeared to want to say something more. "But, sir—"

"Heroes bore the shit out of me," Matt Kincaid said.

"It's not that, sir. It's that I want to make up for my idiocy. I'm not looking to be a hero."

Matt Kincaid reflected for a moment, then came to a decision. "Mr. Taylor, I can say that my experience is a good bit more than yours. I am older than you and I've been in this army longer. Let me tell you, one of the best assurances that you will repeat your mistake lies not in wiping it out as you wish to do by some kind of admirable action, but by living with it. That is going to be painful, mister. But that is what will teach you. And only that." And then, following the briefest pause, "That is it, mister!"

Taylor couldn't snap a salute; his arm was much too painful. But he did manage a slow, rubbery movement of his arm. "Yes, sir. Thank you, sir. I think I understand."

Matt Kincaid, his gray eyes cold, hard, as expressionless as granite, was already walking away.

Mr. Taylor stepped into his saddle and swung onto his horse. He motioned the men forward. As he rode out of the meadow he felt terrible. He felt as though his whole world had collapsed, and he could hardly think of Moynihan dead, Furman dying, and the four wounded, nor that look on Matt Kincaid's face when he had asked to stay in the field.

But he knew that Kincaid was right. It angered him to have to accept that, and yet, as he felt how much he wanted to rid himself of his feeling of guilt and stupidity, he knew too that Lieutenant Matt Kincaid was a hell of a lot smarter than he had ever imagined.

When Matt and Windy and the patrol caught up with the Cohoes cattle, they found the army detail guarding the herd right along with some of the cowboys. It drew a lot of bantering from their Easy Company companions.

Windy coughed out a laugh as he sized up the situation. "Bet you soldier boys never knew you'd end up punching beeves, did you?" And he dropped an eyelid as he rode up to Private Eddie Anders, who had been assigned by Taylor.

Anders, a young man with sandy hair and a wide-open face, broke into a big grin. "It sure ain't like soldiering, Mr. Mandalian."

And Windy laughed at that; he didn't know anyone who called him Mr. Mandalian, except now and again Kincaid or Conway, in jest.

Cohoes and Domino were no more sociable than they had been the last time Matt saw them.

"I am aiming to push up to the shipping point with the herd, Kincaid. Could use some of your men to help us with them red bastards that I hear are running all over the country butchering good honest citizens."

"Cohoes, it is not the time to move up into that country. The Brulés are out in force and I would not advise it. I can leave men with you only if you remain where you are, but if you push to the Stinking Water you'll be asking for big trouble."

128

"I am not aiming to sit here, Kincaid, just picking my nose!"

"Sorry, Cohoes."

"Sorry, my ass," cut in Ching Domino, stomping up and catching the last words. "Sorry about them sheep, are you? How about them sheep coming into good grazing ground—cattle country—and ruining it? Hell, you got ranchers in this here, and now you be letting them Basque bastards come in with their fuckin' sheep!"

Kincaid turned a hard look on the big foreman, waiting a moment before responding, "We're not looking for a cattle and sheep war, Domino. The sheepmen will be told where they can graze their woollies, and so will the cattlemen know where they can run their stock. But get one thing clear, this will not be on tribal land."

Cohoes's face had turned a dark red, the lines on his furious jaw looking like hatchet marks. "You're not telling me you'll let sheep in here, into this graze! I mean to bring up more herds, and so do other drovers, by God!"

"I am not telling you anything, Cohoes," said Matt, and there was a glitter in his eyes. "I just told you."

Domino suddenly spat furiously at the ground, just in front of himself. "You know how them disgustin' sheep bastards castrate them animals, do you?"

"That I do."

"Not with a knife, like normal folks cuttin' horses or bulls. Shit, no. They do it by *bitin'* their nuts off with their fuckin' teeth!"

"Say..." Windy unwound himself from the side of the chuckwagon. "Say, you want to know how a Sioux castrates a Texas cattleman?"

Ching Domino and Cohoes turned furious glares on the scout, whose face was washed in complete innocence.

"Easy," Windy went on, his voice soft as powder. "Easy. That wild Injun just castrates the cattleman with the cattleman's own teeth."

Cohoes and Domino were so outraged at the scout that they were speechless.

"We'll be in the area," Kincaid said, stepping into the lethal tableau.

Cohoes found his voice. "You taking your men?"

"For now. There are ranchers who need support. We'll be patrolling between here and the Haymaker outfit on Jack Creek. Not too far."

Without anything more being said, Kincaid turned and walked toward his horse, Windy following.

Very often, the long view over the plain seemed to shimmer, and perspective was tricky. The horse and rider now appeared indistinguishable from the clump of willows. Only in movement, as they broke out of the horizon, did they become clear.

They moved slowly, the rider watching carefully for sign, noting the jay creasing the sky as it plunged out of a stand of box elders near the river. The rider's whole body sharpened. Shifting in his dark brown saddle, he eased the holstered .45 at his right hip, and touched the hideout gun under his shirt. Yet he did not alter the slow, picking gait of the little dun gelding.

In a few moments he was in cover again, and he drew rein. Now he saw the coyote running and knew why the jay had been startled. Still, he kept at the alert. Reaching to the pocket of his faded blue shirt, he took out a cheroot and lighted it, striking the wooden lucifer on the saddlehorn. But he didn't throw the match, he put it back into his shirt pocket.

Seen close now, he was a stocky, muscular man of medium height, still young, yet with the marks of years in his face. His blue eyes were widely spaced, and at their corners could be seen the faint imprint of crow's-feet. He crossed his arms now, leaning forward onto the pommel of the saddle, peering out from the protection of the thin trees to study the trail ahead.

He had seen the army patrol riding away from the herd, and wondered if they had left more men behind, or had possibly taken back those who were already there. He would check that later, toward evening, when the light would be more in his favor.

He drew on his cheroot. It was good. It had been a long wait, and he knew he was getting restless and would have to be careful. He had not dared to show himself in the town, and so he'd had to live off the land. Good enough, except for nothing to drink, and no women or cards. What was more, hunting was difficult, for he only had the two handguns. But he had earned a satisfaction; he had figured right on Cohoes and Domino bringing the herd up the Greybull to the Stinking Water. That was a gamble he had won.

He leaned back in the saddle, his hand automatically reaching to his other shirt pocket; only the deck was not there. He wondered if the Indian had been found. More than likely. Well, there was nothing there that would identify himself. He had not tarried after the shooting—that cheating son of a bitch—he had not even waited to collect the deck of cards. Nor had he left any trace with the first featherhead, the one who'd been packing in that fresh-shot elk. But the fool had argued with a hungry man, and he should've known better. Anyhow, dead men tell no tales, and that was the big point.

Well, it shouldn't be too long now. They'd be within range of the depot soon, and he'd have to make his play before that. And then, by God, he'd have that herd—his herd, most of it his—what that bastard Domino had stolen while he was in the pen, and was now partnering with Elihu Cohoes.

Yes, his plan was clean. He'd let them trail the herd pretty close to the Stinking Water and he'd just take it— for they weren't expecting him, not by a long shot, with fifteen years' sentence next to his name. He had considered waiting until the beeves were sold and then simply taking the money, but it would have had to be in town, with any number of witnesses and other possibilities that might work against him. No, this was safer. He knew he could handle the men. Ching Domino would have it all pretty well organized, and he would simply step in and take over. He had planned it close. It was going to work. It had to work.

By God, he had tried the straight side of the law. He'd gotten himself together that herd of beeves, worked like hell for it, rounding up mavericks and whatever else he could lay an iron on down in the brakes around Harleyville. His plan had been to make a stake and maybe then send for the kid to come help him out with running a few head. But he had lost half the herd to that sonofabitch Domino in a game of stud, and then the next thing they were partners; until the law from that old robbery at Medicine Bow had caught up with him and he'd been taken. Well, he was out, and Ching Domino and Cohoes had taken the herd. And he was coming to get his. Larrabee Hogan was coming to get what was his.

fifteen ⎯⎯⎯⎯⎯⎯⎯⎯⎯

Otio brought her cheese and goat's milk and some meat. She looked with suspicion at the meat, and raised her eyes inquiringly as he squatted near.

"Xarkia," he said.

She held it to her nose, wrinkling her face a little.

"It is mutton jerky," Xerxes told her from the other side of the tent, where he had been changing the dressing on his arm. "Otio, you must learn the English better."

"I will learn Indian," Otio said. Then, to the girl, "It is from the *ardiak,* the sheep."

She was shaking her head.

He shrugged and handed her a piece of garlic. "You want?"

She shook her head; she had tried it the day before.

"Wine?" He studied her. "What you want?"

She said nothing, just ate the cheese slowly, her eyes cast down.

"We move the sheep again," he said. "Can you walk this time?" And he pointed to her leg.

"Walk?"

"If it hurts bad, you can ride the mule. But better to walk."

He stood up as Ciriaco and Little Marc entered. "We move them."

"In what direction?" Ciriaco asked. "We move closer to the soldiers or away from them?"

They had stepped outside the tent, and Otio said, "Over on the other side of that rise."

133

"There is the timber."

"Yes, and it will take too long to go around it. I looked this morning with Moro."

"But we will have trouble going through the trees. It will be too hard for the sheep, will it not?" said Ciriaco.

"We will do what we did last time, in the Sierra. You remember?"

Ciriaco raised his eyebrows. Ah, yes, he remembered well. "That will be good. That is the good way to do it." He was about to say more when all at once they heard horses approaching.

"It is the soldiers," someone called as Otio grabbed his rifle.

Still with the weapon in his hand, he walked forward to where one of the dogs was sitting, its tongue hanging out, tail bouncing expectantly.

Otio recognized Windy Mandalian instantly, and Ciriaco let out a great shout of welcome, running toward the scout with his knees wobbling, his hands almost touching the ground, with a grotesque limp, as though he were some sort of wild animal.

"Good thing I looked at you twice," Windy said with a big grin. "I was about to plug me a crazy-looking bear."

The watching herders roared with laughter.

"A wild animal," laughed Ciriaco.

"Or a wild human—more dangerous," Otio said.

"This here is Lieutenant Kincaid; I told you about him," Windy said nodding toward Matt.

"I've heard a lot about you," Matt said, "and I'm happy we finally meet, though the circumstances could be better."

"Circum—eh?" Otio looked toward his uncle for help.

Ciriaco was standing at rigid attention, and now whipped a blinding salute at Matt Kincaid, who returned it laughing. Windy had told him about Ciriaco.

"He tells that he wishes there was no Indian fighting," Ciriaco explained to Otio, who suddenly remembered Morning Flower in the tent.

"Julio, bring some food and coffee for the visitors. We go to Xerxes's tent."

"Xerxes?" But Ciriaco's words died when he saw the warning look on Otio's face.

Only they were not quick enough. Xerxes, who was a bit hard of hearing, caught only part of what Otio had said, and from force of habit stepped into the first tent, holding the flap for Kincaid and Windy.

"They will take the girl, it is sure," Ciriaco whispered, and Otio almost kicked him, for the whisper was like a trumpet. Ready to face the worst, he entered with Ciriaco.

But the girl was not there. There was the bedding, and the rugs, boxes, and panniers—and of course the men.

"We will go to Xerxes's tent," Otio said, this time loud enough for Xerxes to hear. "It will be more comfortable. And that is where I told Julio to bring the food and coffee."

But Julio at that moment ducked into the tent carrying bread and cheese and the wineskin.

"The coffee will come," he said. "I did not hear if you wanted wine, Otio."

"Yes. If the visitors wish some." He turned to Kincaid and Windy. "Wine? You wish wine?"

"Not for me," Matt said.

"He don't drink," Windy said, accepting the offer for himself. "Except when he ain't on duty."

Matt said, "We are asking that everyone come in closer to the post, since there's no telling when you might get hit again."

"We are already moving in your direction," Otio said. "And we do not need protection. We will be able to drive away the attack. Windy here is welcome, but all those men on horseback will frighten the sheep."

"You better listen to the Lieutenant, Otio," Windy said. "He knows what he's talking about."

"And Otio, my friend, knows what he is talking about. The sheep do not like a lot of strangers with them."

"The thing is," Matt explained, "if Quick Thunder can be stopped right away, then we're all right. But if he gets the idea that he's winning something, if he feels we're in trouble, then he'll get other tribes to come in with him."

"Other tribes?"

"That's the way it works," Windy said.

"We will move closer," Otio said. "We wish to see the graze on the other side of the timber over there."

"I can leave you some men."

Otio shook his head, and said nothing. He had already told them no; why did they keep asking?

When they had gone, Ciriaco said, "Where is the girl?"

"Under the blankets."

Otio walked over and began pulling away the pile of blankets at the end of the tent. Morning Flower lay curled on her side, her arm covering her head.

"You could have gone with the soldiers," Otio said. "They would not have hurt you. The lieutenant would send you back to your people."

"Is that so sure?"

"I think he is an honest man."

"The soldiers always lie. And if they don't lie, then the one above them lies—their soldier chief."

Otio studied it. "Maybe it is so. Yes. I do not trust them so much; but the lieutenant and Windy I trust."

"When will you let me go?"

"When we leave this place."

"You did not kill me," Morning Flower said. "You have not done a bad thing to me."

As they rode away fom the sheep camp, Windy said, "Independent cuss, ain't he?"

Matt nodded. "I like him. I trust him."

"He's all balls," Windy agreed.

"What do you think, Windy?"

"I think the right smart and right now thing is to find out who killed them two Sioux."

"I agree with that. Got any ideas?"

"First thing I want to do is go back and study them tracks again where you and me looked."

"You'll take Henry Walks Quickly with you?"

Windy grinned. "Unless you want to come along."

"I wish I could. I'd much rather, to tell you the truth."

Windy's grin broadened. "Tell you what. I could take along that Ciriaco feller; he's that good at imitatin', he could make like he was you, and I wouldn't feel so lonesome."

sixteen _____

"But we cannot take the time," Otio was saying. "I already told you. We will take a day to circle that stand of timber, and we will run weight off the sheep."

"What then?" Xerxes asked. "If we wish to move down to the river?"

"We must go through the trees."

"But how?" Michel asked. "The trees and the under-brush are too thick. The sheep cannot get through."

Otio looked at Ciriaco.

Ciriaco nodded. "But is it all right with the soldiers? When we fired the timber in the Sierras, it was not in the Wyoming land, but in Nevada. It could be different here."

"It will only burn the brush, clear the way so the sheep can pass. And it is not on the land of the tribes."

"It will not be too difficult to control," Xerxes said, nodding his big head. "We have men, shovels, and axes."

Otio picked up his *makhila*. "We will start the fire there . . . and over there . . . and in the middle," he said, pointing with the walking stick that had been his father's.

"Yes," said Ciriaco. "It will save much time and wear on the sheep."

Windy Mandalian and Henry Walks Quickly moved care-fully along the trail, following the prints left by the lone horseman trailing the cattle herd. But now they had come to a ford at the river, and while they picked up the cattle tracks and those of the drovers' horses on the other side, the horse with the loose shoe had vanished.

"More than likely he rode up or downstream so's nobody could cut his trail," Windy said. "Figuring him for the kind of man he's got to be, he'd be that cautious."

Henry Walks Quickly grunted. He was studying a small chokecherry bush.

"What you got there, Henry?" Windy said, catching something in the Delaware's attitude.

Walks Quickly held up a small piece of cloth.

"Looks to be part of a shirt, I'd say." Windy turned it over.

"Not cowboy," Walks Quickly said.

Windy nodded. "Too slick material for a working cowhand, I'll agree. Fancy stuff. Could be our man." He bent down, peering at a little clump of grass that was bent over at the roots. Some of the grass had been torn from the sod. "It's him. See, that loose shoe done that."

They rode even more slowly now, their eyes keen on the trail they were following, but also wary of any possibility of hostiles suddenly appearing. Now the tracks were clearer.

"Ground is softer," Windy said, "and I know we're getting right close to the place they was holding the herd." He looked at the horizon. "And we're by God getting kind of close to them woollies. Shit." He spat swiftly as his roan horse bent down to bite at a tick on its leg. "Why you figger he don't make his play?"

As was often his habit, Windy liked to talk things over with himself, speaking partly aloud, partly in whisper, or with a kind of muttering. It was how he thought things out. "Son of a bitch is sure up to no good," he muttered. "But what? It can't be a holdup. They don't carry money on those cattle drives. It's got to be either the cows or someone with the herd, some person. Cohoes? Domino? Or somebody else?" He looked at Walks

Quickly. "Is he a lawman? Or a owlhooter?"

In another hour the tracks grew fainter. Windy dismounted and took a close look. "Yep. He's pulled the loose shoe. Probably chucked it a distance. Don't matter, he'll have three on and one off now. Easy to follow."

"We track him," Walks Quickly said.

"Where would you want to face a couple of sweet fellers like Cohoes and Domino, if you was this feller, anxious to settle something?" Windy had not asked the question directly to Walks Quickly, but had muttered it to himself, squinting a little, as though an answer might be somewhere in the atmosphere.

The Indian grunted.

"It'd have to be someplace 'fore they reach the Stinking Water," Windy said. "And that means pretty damn soon."

They had ridden about another hour when Walks Quickly suddenly drew rein. He turned to look at Windy, sniffing.

"You're right," the scout said. "It's smoke."

Walks Quickly was looking to the west.

"It'll be that stand of timber over past Jack Creek," Windy said. "And that is in direct line with the sheep."

"We go look?"

"We better. I dunno if Matt will see it, but we sure better check." And he reined the roan's head in the direction of the smoke and kicked him into a fast trot.

It was the cattle who told the cowboys of the fire. The wind, which was slight, had carried the smell of smoke, and it was in their eyes, their nostrils. And they were instantly restive.

"What goddamn fool is burnin' up the prairie?" Ching Domino demanded.

Cohoes stood hard beside him, his eyes on the cattle

as Heavy Bill Haines and the men mounted up and rode toward the edges of the herd. "Wind can carry that damn thing down here and cut across the prairie quicker'n a cat can lick his ass."

He had just spoken those words when a hand who had been out on picket came riding up.

"Mr. Cohoes, Bill Haines told me to let you know he thinks that's where the sheep is."

"In the fire?"

"Someone saw sheepshit up there by that butte when he went over this morning to look at what he thought was a herd of elk."

"And it was sheep! Why didn't anyone tell me?"

"Visco seen it, and he thought it was elk shit. But he was talking to Heavy Bill just now, and Bill thinks it's the sheep."

Heavy Bill Haines came riding in to where Cohoes and Domino and the hand were talking. Reining hard, he said, "I'm guessing it, but I'd say that's where the sheep are."

"You seen 'em?"

"I said I'm guessing."

Cohoes spat angrily, almost hitting Ching Domino's boot. "Jorgensen, you take the glasses and ride up that there draw and see what you can. I don't want those fucking sheep anywhere near this feed, goddammit!"

He turned to Heavy Bill Haines. "Move 'em down closer to the river."

"I got all hands in the saddle," the trail boss said.

"Keep 'em there." He looked at the big man on the black horse. "Those sheepherders are the dumbest fucking sons of bitches I ever seen by God in this real good while! Settin' fire like that! Goddammit! Goddammit!" He suddenly plunged his hand at his crotch, scratching hard. "Domino, we'll go have a look-see."

seventeen ─────────

The first sergeant of Easy Company was taking a breather. He had finished making up the company duty roster, always a laborious enterprise, for the company was shorthanded, and Ben Cohen never stinted his responsibilities regarding the men's details. Indeed, the sergeant spent exquisite care on the assignment of these important duties, especially the ones known as the "shit details"; these received the full weight of his lengthy experience. But for the present, his immediate task was accomplished and he was able to relax and enjoy a few moments of the late afternoon of a cloudless day. But not for long.

Ben Cohen had been reflecting on the pleasures of a beer or two at the sutler's, when the soldier standing before him came suddenly and rudely into focus.

"What is it, Golightly?" The tone was neutral, yet laced with warning.

"Sarge, I'm all recovered from the piles."

"Congratulations."

"I mean, I'm feeling real fine now, Sarge."

"I heard you the first time, soldier. Tell me what the hell you want!"

Billy Golightly had met his share of tough characters, but he had never encountered anyone like the first sergeant of Easy Company. Ben Cohen was something more than just tough. There was a directness about him that was like a shovel stuck right in your mouth.

"Sarge, I want to get back with the platoon. Is there

any way I could meet up with the patrol ... or something?" He felt the dismay in his voice as he realized the stupidity of his request. Billy Golightly was furious with himself for revealing once again how green he was.

But the expected demolition was not forthcoming.

"Why?" The single word, simple, innocent even, was freighted with danger.

Billy almost stammered. "Sarge, I like it around here, it's fine, but I just want to get into some action. I keep thinking of my buddies out there and ..." Again, there came the sensation of creeping paralysis as his voice trailed off.

The sergeant had been leaning just slightly against the wall outside the orderly room, and now suddenly he straightened and stood planted right in front of Golightly. "Something go wrong with you and your girlfriend, did it?"

"Girlfriend, Sarge?"

"Golightly, cut the shit. I am not blind. You been mooning around here the last day or two like you had a cloud up your ass."

Billy Golightly started to open his mouth to speak, but he closed it. Sergeant Cohen regarded him with eyes of stone.

"Thing is, Sarge, I don't have no girlfriend."

"Come off it, Golightly."

"Sarge, I did have, but I don't anymore, is what I am saying."

Ben Cohen folded his arms across his chest. "How come?" He sniffed, cutting his eye toward the guest barracks. "Not good enough for a delegate's daughter, that it?"

Billy sighed; he was dismayed that Sergeant Cohen— and who else?—had noticed his feelings for Julie Thatcher.

"I guess so, Sarge. She, uh, she seems to prefer that freighter feller."

"That stringbean in the baggy overalls, looks like he's carrying a packsaddle in his crotch?"

Billy nodded, his eyes downcast with rejection as he thought of the bright moments with Julie and how it had all been shattered when that son of a bitch had pulled in.

Sergeant Cohen released an enormous sigh, and for a moment Billy Golightly was drawn to him in an astonishing way, for he felt himself swept by the feeling that the sergeant could help him, could suddenly fix his situation with some all-powerful order. It was a fleeting emotion, but it left him with a new way of looking at Ben Cohen. And suddenly he was no longer afraid of him.

Billy Golightly waited for his first sergeant to say something. But whatever Ben Cohen might have been about to utter never came out, for a shout from the tower guard cut through the late afternoon and brought a new note to the somnolent army outpost.

"Rider coming in fast! Looks to be one of the Delawares! No . . . shit, it's Windy Mandalian!"

The couple writhing together on Julie Thatcher's bed in the guest quarters were totally unaware of the excitement that suddenly gripped Outpost Number Nine at the galloping appearance of the chief scout.

Miss Thatcher and Mr. Venable were wholly absorbed in the renewal of their relationship. Contrary to Julie's fears when she had seen Harry Venable across the parade upon his arrival the previous day, the young man was delighted to see her again. He was in fact giving physical affirmation to his feeling right now, for the third time.

As they slowly returned to consciousness, they became aware of sounds outside on the parade.

"Sounds like something's going on," Harry said, sitting up on the bed.

"Harry . . ."

"Yeah?"

"Come here."

"I just want to see what the ruckus is about."

He stood up and pulled on his overalls.

"Harry, don't get dressed. Come back to bed."

"Be right there."

She watched his back, the sagging crotch of his overalls, as he crossed to the window and looked out.

"Looks like some excitement," he said. "I better find out what it is—might be something to do with my team and wagon, or who knows what."

"Harry . . ."

He walked over to her and sat on the edge of the bed. "Obliged for the nice time," he said. "I'd like to come again." He gave a little laugh at his own joke.

"Harry, you're sweet." She held her eyes on his long, thin profile, wondering.

His eyes were on her breasts. "You're still beautiful," he said. "I had a talk with your dad. Thought we might get hitched."

"You mean . . . married?"

"I don't mean let's go for a picnic."

"Harry, that's sweet of you."

"Just say the day."

"Harry . . . I'd like to think it over."

His jaw dropped. "What do you mean, think it over? I thought—"

But he was cut off by a knock at the door.

"Julie, are you in there?" Her father's voice came booming into the room.

"I'll be right out, Father." And swiftly she was on her feet, hurrying into her clothes.

146

As she was about to open the door, Harry Venable said, "Well, what about it, Julie? I thought your old man...I told you I talked to him."

Julie stopped and stood quite still in front of him. "You're a nice fellow, Harry," she said, and a smile started teasing her mouth. "And I'm glad you and Father reached an understanding."

"Julie..."

"I said I'd like to think it over, Mr. Venable."

Hawes Thatcher, however, had grown impatient waiting for his daughter, and he was gone. Julie stepped out onto the parade in time to see Windy Mandalian and Captain Conway crossing to the orderly room, followed by Sergeant Cohen. She was looking to see if Billy was around when the sentry called out.

"First Platoon riding in!"

And she watched the big gate swing open and Lieutenant Matt Kincaid appear on his big horse, leading the soldiers into Outpost Number Nine.

eighteen ⸻

"Well, let's hear it." The commanding officer of Easy Company sat down quickly in his swivel chair and looked at his adjutant and chief scout as he picked up the cold cigar butt from the ashtray and relighted it.

Matt nodded to Windy to speak first. "The herders started a brushfire to clear out some timber so they could drive the woollies through; saved them going around the long way."

"Not on Sioux land, I hope."

"On federal. No, they got it under control. They know what they're doin', as far as the fire is concerned. Only thing is, they're moving right into that area where Cohoes has got his cattle coming up along the river. They are bound to meet, more sooner than later the way they're both going."

"It'll be jolly when they meet," said Conway. "But I can tell you've got more."

This time the scout did not take his time, but spoke right out. "On the way back, me and Henry Walks Quickly almost run smack into a big war party."

"Brulés?" Matt asked, looking over at the scout.

"Brulés. And Hunkpapas and Oglallas."

"That does it," said Conway, slapping the palm of his hand on the desktop.

"Sir," Matt said, "they've already wiped out two of the ranches along the Potterville cutoff—Soames and Piper."

"Bad?"

"As bad as it ever gets."

Conway made a face. "Where were they, Windy?"

"Down near Horsehead Creek. Couldn't tell if they were headed for the sheep, the cattle, or both—or for us here."

"How many?"

"We figured a hundred and fifty. But there could be more. We didn't hang around to take a tally."

Matt grinned. "Sir, I'd like First and Second Platoon. We had better get right out there."

"Taylor and Second Platoon are already alerted, Matt." The captain leaned forward. "When I saw Windy ride in, and you right after, I wasn't looking for good news. You'll not have time to rest."

"We don't need it, Captain."

Conway stood up. "We'll be well covered here with myself, Fletcher, and Third Platoon."

"Yes, sir."

"You know the terrain. You'll make your battle plan as you ride, I expect. Matt, you and Windy are the best we've got. Take care. That is an order."

"Yes, sir."

Windy winked. "I'm going to need a fresh mount, if the United States Army can spare one."

"Consider it done," Captain Conway said, and then, turning his head to the partly opened door, "Sergeant Cohen?"

"Yes, sir?" The first sergeant appeared in the doorway.

"Order up a good horse for Mr. Mandalian here."

"Yes, sir."

"Want to try one of our McClellan saddles, Mr. Chief Scout?"

"I think too much of my balls, thank you, Captain." And he walked out laughing.

Ben Cohen gave the order to Bradshaw, the company clerk. "Get it to the stables, and then send Golightly to me. Fast, Corporal."

In a few minutes, Bradshaw was back with Billy Golightly.

"You asked to get into the field with your platoon, soldier. Here's your opportunity. Git."

"Gee, thanks, Sarge." Billy was so flustered he whipped up a salute and spun on his heel.

"Goddammit, Golightly, I ought to bust your ass right now. I am not a officer. I am your first sergeant and you do not salute me. Goddammit!"

"Sorry, sir . . . I mean, Sergeant!"

"Goddammit, Golightly, how old are you anyway?"

"Sarge, I'm twenty-two."

"Bullshit. I'd say you were twenty-two months, if that. Now get your ass into that saddle—*right now!*"

As they rode out, the blue-and-white guidon fluttered at Matt Kincaid's right, carried by Malone, solid and eager for battle, as always. Reb McBride rode at Kincaid's left.

To the left of First Platoon, Mr. Taylor led the Second. His left-flank outriders were out of Kincaid's view, while the First's right-flankers were not visible to Taylor. Yet the two officers were able to send hand signals to each other, and so they managed to cover a much wider field than either could have done alone. Army regulations called for at least one-third of the company to be kept in reserve and holding the base of operations, and so they had not ridden out full strength.

As they topped a rise about two-thirds of the way to where Cohoes had last been seen with his cattle, Matt spotted Windy Mandalian talking to Henry Walks Quickly. Raising his hand to halt the outfit, Kincaid turned to Gus Olsen and said, "Take over and rest, Sergeant." Then he turned and spurred his mount forward, trotting up to join Windy and the Delaware scout.

"What's up, Windy?"

"Henry's found something on the feller we figure shot them two Brulés."

"Where?"

Walks Quickly nodded his head to Windy.

"He was sayin' he followed more of them tracks that me and him was looking into," the scout said. "The rider was following Cohoes's herd. Now, he'd always keep about the same distance from them. When they stopped, he'd stop. When they pulled out, he pulled out. Smart boy."

"So what do we know from that for sure?" Matt asked.

"We know he only has a handgun, and likely a hideout—one or both."

Walks Quickly opened his hand to show an empty shell. "He was hunting with that—he dropped it. Probably the only mistake he's made so far, but a good one for us. Maybe he's short on ammo. Remember when the first Indian was killed—Young Man Catching Up—there was blood on him that couldn't have been his own, since he was shot clean. I've a notion it was animal—deer or elk, maybe antelope. Suppose he'd killed a elk, say, and this man found him and wanted the meat and Young Man said no. This feller's low on ammo, so he wants to be sure. So he walks away and shoots Young Man in the back. I'm guessing, mind."

"And the other Brulé. Was it the same man?"

"Not sure. But he was white, and there are no buff hunters around right now. Man hiding out on the trail, living off the land, might sure want a little relaxation, so he'd maybe gamble some. He'd lose. But then he might know what gossips some Indians are. Losing could've sobered his thinking some."

"So what do you get from all that?"

"First, it's probably the same person. Second, he's been up in this part of the country ahead of Cohoes and Domino, and waiting for them. And third, he'll be pulling his play about now. My guess is he was double-crossed. Maybe since he's a gambler, he could've lost the herd in a game."

Matt nodded, biting his lower lip. "Hangs together."

"I'm figuring we'll reach Franc's Crossing pretty directly now," Windy said.

"We'll split the command there—First Platoon to the cattle, Second to the sheep. The order will be to hold them away from each other."

"With that fire started by Otio and his boys, that'll be a problem. And then there is old Lo, the poor Indian. He'll be looking for his sweetheart, Revenge, in no uncertain way."

They reached Franc's Crossing about the time that Windy and Matt had figured. Kincaid called a halt and the men let their mounts drink.

They had been there only a little while when suddenly the sound of rifle fire came echoing across the plains.

nineteen _____

The fire had burned itself out, the herders keeping it always under control. Brush had been cleared, and at a suitable moment Otio ordered the band of sheep moved through the cleared timber.

It was a bright morning. The men were in good spirits, for they were saving a lot of time. The girl was able to walk, though her leg did appear to cause her some discomfort. But she did not complain. She ate what was offered her, and she did not converse. She was not antagonistic, however, but simply held her own counsel. Otio and Ciriaco had slackened their efforts to communicate with her. Yet Otio found himself stealing looks every so often, and this did not go unnoticed by an amused Ciriaco.

They had finally passed through the timber, and now Otio stood on a high rise of ground, looking across the swelling prairie as it fell toward the river.

"What do you think, Nephew?" Ciriaco asked. "The feed is only so-so, it seems to me."

"Closer to the river it would be better," Otio replied. But he did not look at his uncle. He was staring at something in the distance.

"What is it?" Ciriaco asked after a moment, catching something in Otio's attitude.

"Horses."

"Ah, I see them."

"And men."

"Yes, men too."

Otio took the field glasses that had been strapped to one of the packmules.

"How many men?" Ciriaco asked.

"I count ten." He lowered the glasses. "And they have guns." He turned quickly. "Michel, bunch the *ardiak*. Take Pinto and Rom, leave the other dogs free. Xerxes, call the men. Hurry!" He turned back to Ciriaco. "I think we have a fight on our hands."

"Fighting?" Ciriaco's eyes were big and round. "Is it the Indians?"

"It looks like the men who drive the cows."

At Outpost Number Nine, Hawes Thatcher stretched his long legs, leaned back in his easy chair, and, with one eyebrow raised, looked down the length of his body to the toe of his boot. He let his eyes move now to the girl sitting across from him.

"I have spoken to Venable, as you know, my dear." The words were soft, couched in a mixture of confiding familiarity and parental authority. "He is not the person, I must say, I'd normally choose for a son-in-law. He is hardly, shall we say, wholly desirable. But he is a man, and he is a husband for you, my dear. And under the circumstances, as the old saying has it, beggars cannot be choosers."

Typically, he did not notice the flush that came to his daughter's cheeks as he said those words, nor how her lips tightened.

"It remains to choose a time and place."

"Yes, Father." Julie Thatcher lowered her eyes to look at her hands lying in her lap. She spoke the words so softly that he barely heard her.

"Are you feeling all right, Julie?"

"Yes I am, Father." She raised her head. "I think I'll go in and lie down."

"Ah, yes, of course, my dear." His smile was filled with paternal understanding, which infuriated her.

But the girl didn't get up right away. She watched her father pick up his newspaper and start to read. It was as though she had already left the room.

Julie Thatcher continued to sit there facing her father's opened newspaper. But she was not thinking of her father. Nor was she thinking of her prospective husband. She was thinking of the young soldier who had shown her the horses and had talked to her about his life, and had held her hand. She was thinking of Billy Golightly.

The object of her attention was presently watching the two Delaware scouts riding in toward First Platoon as fast as their ponies could run. The dry ground thrummed under the racing hooves, the ponies streaked out to their whole length, like racing greyhounds. Where the plain lifted to a ridge, Windy Mandalian and Henry Walks Quickly could be seen sitting their mounts and watching something beyond.

The two Delawares came dashing up to whirl to a dazzling stop in front of Lieutenant Matt Kincaid.

"Windy tell—stay here. Many Sioux ahead. Many. Many Brulés, Hunkpapa, Oglalla. All painted up."

Billy heard Lieutenant Kincaid say, "Shit!" He was sitting his horse close by, and now he remembered hearing a few times since he'd joined the army how it was on a clear day like this that General George Armstrong Custer had only recently led the Seventh Cavalry right smack into the middle of a vast Indian trap. Sitting up a little straighter in his saddle, Billy reflected on the mutilated bodies, the torn heads dripping with blood that had been found near the Little Big Horn—not so very far from where Easy Company's First Platoon now waited. A very strange sensation began to creep along

Billy Golightly's spine and up into his scalp.

Presently, Windy Mandalian and Henry Walks Quickly rode back to the platoon.

"There's a good two hundred," Billy heard the scout say. "Quick Thunder's hooked up with more Oglallas and Hunkpapas. Matt, we had best backtrack and head across by Slim Butte; try to get to the cattle ahead of them."

"I'm sending a man back to warn Captain Conway," Kincaid said. "It's two hundred now; it could get to be a whole lot more if they start feeling they're getting us on the run."

"That I know. That I know."

Suddenly, Billy heard his name called.

"Yes, sir." He kneed his mount toward Lieutenant Kincaid.

"Ride back to Number Nine and inform Captain Conway that we've sighted about two hundred Sioux, though we've not made contact so far. We're going around by Slim Butte to try to reach the Cohoes herd ahead of them. Since they don't seem to be in any hurry, we've got a chance. How's your horse?" Kincaid had spoken fast, and Billy knew he wasn't going to repeat anything; but he made an extra effort to get the message exactly.

"He's good, sir. Got good wind. We'll make it."

"Good luck."

Billy snapped a salute, wheeled his horse, and was racing back down the way they had come.

Larrabee Hogan rode slowly out of the clump of box elders and toward the cowboy lounging in his saddle at the edge of the cattle herd.

"Howdy."

The rider, looking up, greeted Hogan with a nod, exhibiting the usual wary neutrality of the trail.

"I am heading toward the Stinking Water cattle depot," Hogan said, reaching into his shirt pocket for a cheroot. "Got a light, have you?"

The cowboy, wearing a dusty brown Stetson hat with a piece torn out of the brim, bent his head slightly as he reached for a lucifer. And Larrabee Hogan laid the barrel of his .45 easily along the back of that bent head.

Then, holding his victim so he wouldn't fall out of the saddle, he led his horse back into the box elders. Here the unconscious cowboy fell to the ground as Hogan released him. Swiftly he bound him with strips of rawhide and the cowboy's own lariat and gagged him tightly with a piece of his shirt.

"You'll sleep awhile," he said softly. "And when you wake up you'll have a new boss."

According to his reckoning, there were four more men with the herd; he had seen the others ride out. If he could take them at gunpoint, he could pull it off. And to add to his good fortune, the man he had knocked out had a Winchester in his saddle boot.

twenty _____

Now, as the cowboys approached, Otio decided to change his tactics, and he ordered the sheep to start down toward the river. This caused a certain amount of consternation among the herders.

"They do not want the sheep near the cows," Xerxes said.

"They do not like the sheep," observed Ciriaco.

"It is not for them to like or not like." Otio's tone was angry; and he stood there on the slope, stubborn as old Yanni, one of the bull-jawed lead goats famous back in the Sierras. "The lieutenant said we could go on the federal land, and this is the federal land, and down there too, where we plan to go. He said so."

"But Otio..."

There was no moving him, and they knew it, and so their argument had no force. Now the dogs, led by Moro, moved swiftly and the sheep started down toward the river.

"They will learn, those cattlemen, that the land is for all," Otio said defiantly.

It was a barely perceptible slope, and in a few moments the dogs had the sheep spread out like a great carpet over the prairie.

But the horsemen, seeing the maneuver, started riding to head off the sheep, yelling, waving their hats, and cracking the ends of their lariat ropes like whips.

"Hey you—you stop!" shouted Otio, and the other herders took it up, yelling at the cowboys to leave the sheep alone. But the sheepmen were outmaneuvered, for the cowboys were on horseback, and the herders' mules were no match for those cattle ponies.

The more the herders yelled at them, the more the cowboys raced among the sheep, terrifying them, chasing the scurrying, scrambling woollies over the prairie, while they roared with glee at the fun they were having.

Suddenly a rifle shot wiped out all that laughter, as one of the horsebackers clutched his arm, hardly remaining in his saddle.

"I wound you only," Otio shouted. "As warning. Next shoot—I kill! Get out!"

But almost before he'd finished, the cowboys were firing at the sheepmen. Old Enrique was nicked along his right buttock, which brought from the old man a crescendo of oaths. But Otio accounted for the man he had intentionally wounded, his next bullet going through the cowboy's stomach. And Ciriaco toppled the man riding next to him.

The cowboys had whipped back out of range now, and were conferring.

"Wipe the sons of bitches plumb out!" ordered Ching Domino. "Try and save those fucking woollies, though; we can sell them."

Cohoes had been chewing pretty vigorously on the wooden match in his mouth, and now, without touching it with his hand, he switched it to the other side of his face. "Take it slow a minute. See that big bastard who shot Collins? He's their leader. He's the one to get. Now then, fan out. Run your horses straight at the sons of bitches. Then, just when you get in range, split into three groups—one right down the middle, the other two on each side. I want every damn one of them sheepshitters taken care of. But get that big bastard first. With him gone, they'll be easy."

By now the herders had left the sheep to the dogs to handle, and had retreated back to the timber, finding good cover. Xerxes had been hit in the same arm that had been wounded in the fight with Quick Thunder and the Sioux.

"Lucky I am," he said. "The arm was not being used anyway."

On the cowpunchers' first charge, Otio was nicked along the back of his hand. But he dropped one of the attackers, and it made the riders cautious. They rode back to where Cohoes—still not using a gun—was waiting for them.

"We are getting noplace fast," Ching Domino announced angrily. "That big son of a bitch could knock the balls off a eagle chasing his girl friend, for Chrissake."

"How are we on ammo?"

They counted enough to conclude the fight if they could knock off the sheepherders' leader.

"We'll send back to the chuckwagon if need be," Cohoes said, his Adam's apple pumping up and down fast, "and bring in some more of the boys—except I don't like to draw men away from the herd. Shit, we're down two, and Harrigan is hit in the leg, to boot. And Murray's got a crease across his back."

"Shit take it," muttered Ching Domino.

Elihu Cohoes squinted at the sun. "That grass would go like the wind if a man set a match to it. And it is blowin' right in their direction. Any of you men favor roast mutton?"

Kincaid and his men had successfully avoided confrontation with the Sioux, and had drawn back to where it was possible to branch off on another trail that would lead to the cattle herd.

"Might turn to our advantage them two gettin' their

stock close together," Windy said as they trotted down a long draw. "They won't be so spread out, and the Sioux can't pick them off so easy."

"Thing is to get to the herd before Quick Thunder, in any case," said Matt. "I don't think he's especially anxious at this stage to tangle with the army; though if he gets some more followers, he'll try to wipe us out."

"He wants the sheep and cattle first; and you're right there," Windy agreed.

It was less than an hour later that they heard rifle fire off their left flank.

"That'll be the cattle or the sheep, one or t'other" Windy said. "We better push it."

Matt was already giving the order to lift the pace.

When they were closer, they drew rein, Matt raising his arm in signal to the platoon. The firing was louder; it seemed to be coming from over the ridge right in front of them.

"Sioux, would you say, Windy?"

"Don't believe so. Don't hear no whooping and chanting."

"Sounds like Spencers," Matt said in another moment.

"I'd say it was the herders locking horns with their cattle buddies." The scout chuckled. "Jesus, the Sioux'll let them just knock each other off and then they'll sashay in, counting coup pretty as you please."

Matt raised his arm and the horses started off quickly, in a moment breaking into a fast trot. As they cut down the long side of the draw, he lifted the tempo. They were going at a good clip as they swept up toward the lip of the draw and the rifle fire grew louder.

Just as they reached the crest, there came a tremendous crashing of gunfire and they heard the cries of the warriors, who they now saw breaking across the plain toward the cattlemen and sheepherders.

"Guide on my right and on my left," Kincaid ordered,

and the platoon poured across the hard ground. Just within rifle range, Matt ordered a halt.

"Sergeant Olsen, give the order to dismount and proceed on foot toward the flanks of the engagement. Extra caution not to hit any whites!"

The Sioux, led by Quick Thunder and Wound, along with a Hunkpapa and an Oglalla chief, were numerous, greatly outnumbering the cattlemen and herders—and, Kincaid wryly decided, outmanning the army as well. But where was Taylor?

Strangely, as though reading his mind, Windy said, "Where do you reckon Taylor got to? He was supposed to meet the herders, right?"

Matt nodded. "Right. But he may have run into something with one of the ranchers. We already know Quick Thunder and his boys were dropping in."

Suddenly a shout went up, and Olsen called out to Kincaid, "Lieutenant, the grass is fired!"

The flames were not high, but the fire was spreading fast, the slight wind blowing it from the cattlemen toward the herders. The sheep had started to panic at the smell. And now, during a lull in the firing, the combatants watched the flames as the fire, started by Cohoes, raced across the ground.

"It is time for us to haul ass," Cohoes announced to his men.

Ching Domino was reluctant to leave their quarry, who seemed to be using the cattlemen and their horses for shooting practice.

Cohoes, trying to top Domino's earlier description of Otio's shooting, now said, "Bastard could shoot the button off your shirt without cutting the thread."

"We could whistle up some more of our boys," Ching Domino said.

Cohoes was shaking his head, his eyes on the spreading fire. "Thing is the cattle. We got to get them to market. Fuck this here. Let 'em have it for now. We got to ship them beeves. Let the goddamn army settle it."

Billy Golightly delivered his message to Captain Warner Conway, and for a few great moments something inside him said he was a hero. The glory was brief. Sergeant Ben Cohen scowled and made some remark about his piles, and the sight of his hated rival, Harry Venable, lounging outside the sutler's lowered his spirits even more. There was no sign of Julie Thatcher, to his dismay; for even though he had lost her to that skinny freighter, his dreams of glory, his eagerness for the ride, had all been for her.

"Be doubly careful going back," Captain Conway cautioned him. "You've delivered your message, and the tendency is to relax. Don't lower your guard. Get it?"

"Yes, sir. I'll be extra careful, sir."

"We need every man at this point," said Conway.

"You can count on me, sir."

Billy rode fast back to where he had left First Platoon, exercising extra care as he approached the cattle herd. He was no stranger to cautious movement. His elder brother had taught him. And so, not riding straight in, he circled the herd, working his way closer.

He was surprised not to find the army there, but he could hear distant gunfire, not close enough to spook the cattle, but still, if it came closer, there could be trouble with a couple thousand head stampeding. The real funny thing was that he only saw three riders. He wondered if the others were at the fighting, though he assumed some riders must be on the far side of the herd. But who was fighting? Was First Platoon up there?

He noted that the cattle appeared to be in good condition; they'd bring a healthy dollar to Cohoes.

Billy Golightly had stepped down from his horse to tighten the cinch, and in fact had his back toward the voice that now spoke.

"Well, if it ain't the little soldier boy."

Billy had the stirrup of his McClellan up on his shoulder while he unbuckled and then tightened the cinch, and now he dropped it, turning to face the man who had spoken.

"Real slow-like."

Billy stood facing Ching Domino and the man beside him, Elihu Cohoes, the man with the one eye. But his attention was really on Domino, who had spoken to him in the Silver Tip saloon the day of the fight with the cowboys, and who had stared at him the time he'd ridden out to the herd with Lieutenant Kincaid. And again he wondered why he'd been stared at that way, why the man called Domino had asked him in the saloon if he hadn't seen him somewhere before.

"What you doing here, soldier?" Cohoes said.

"I was figuring to meet up with my platoon. You been up at the fighting?"

"You can see they ain't here," Ching Domino said with a sneer.

"They up yonder? You come from the fighting?" Billy asked again.

"They are up there," Cohoes said, "along with them sheepshitters and screaming Indians." He swung toward the man beside him. "Domino, we got to get out of here before that hash is settled and someone starts looking for these beeves."

"See you gents later," Billy said, moving toward his horse.

"Not so fast, young soldier. Not so fast."

"What the hell you doing?" Billy found himself staring at the big Navy Colt in Ching Domino's fist.

167

"You'll keep us company," Cohoes said. "Just in case we need some insurance."

The other men who had been at the fighting with Cohoes and Domino had all moved in closer now and dismounted, and were standing there waiting for orders.

"Drop your gunbelt." Elihu Cohoes rubbed the side of his nose with his thumb knuckle.

"The army will catch you up for this," Billy said.

"I said drop it!"

"What the hell do you want with me?" But he was already unbuckling his belt.

There was a sharp grin on Ching Domino's face. "On account of we like you—Mr. Hogan."

And while the shock hit Billy with a rush of blood to his face, Cohoes turned his head and barked at the men to get fresh mounts fast and start the herd moving.

But those words had hardly been spoken when a new voice came from the screen of trees lining a part of the river behind the spot where Billy was standing.

"I have got you all covered, and know this—I can shoot the asshole out of a drunk prairie dog, standing on my head!"

Ching Domino's hand had moved, still holding the Navy Colt, but he did not pull the trigger.

"No!" the voice commanded. Then, "That's better, Domino."

And now Billy knew who it was.

"Kid, take their guns. You men drop your belts. I mean right now. And Cohoes, in case you're wondering, your men are here with me. Any of you want to argue it, like one of them did, can also end up permanent here. Billy, get their guns."

"Larry . . . is that you?" Billy had turned to look, but the man who had spoken was still hidden in the trees.

"Who the hell did you think it was? I'm mighty surprised to see you, boy. Heard you joined the army, but didn't know I'd have this good luck. I can use a trusted buddy, let me tell you." And Billy listened to the familiar chuckle.

"Get their guns, boy."

Billy hesitated.

"Kid . . ."

"Larry, I dunno."

"What the hell do you mean, you don't know!" The voice was suddenly hard as a board.

"I'm a soldier now, Larry. I dunno about this."

"Billy, I am telling you to pick up those guns. You men step away from those belts. Step back, and I do mean right now!"

And now they all saw him as he stepped out from the protection of the trees. They all saw the Winchester .44-40.

"Billy, do what I tell you. You're not talking to your brother now, you're talking to Larrabee Hogan."

The sheepmen were well forted in the timber, and Otio's accuracy had impressed the Sioux as it had the cattlemen. Matt Kincaid had deployed his platoon skillfully against the hostiles, but the withdrawal of the Cohoes guns had been unfortunate. The Sioux outnumbered them heavily.

Early in the fight, Kincaid had sent Windy and Henry Walks Quickly to locate Taylor, but as yet he'd received no news. The platoon had suffered three dead and six wounded; the Indians had taken more losses than that, for they had been fighting in the open, charging in, showing their bravery as was their way, thus exposing themselves to the prone soldiers, the forted-up herders, and especially Otio Esteban.

"Uncle, we need to watch the ammunition, it is getting low."

169

"I know." Ciriaco looked gloomy. "Those redskins, they fight like hell."

"So do we sheepherders, Uncle."

Ciriaco grinned.

"How is Michel?"

"He was hit again. But he is all right," Ciriaco said. "I wish I could say the same for Tonio." And his eyes filled.

"Tonio fought well, Uncle, and died well. We must be happy for him."

"It is true. I go count the ammunition. Kill some more of the red bastards, Otio."

He had only checked the girl once. For the most part she had remained under cover. Otio had half expected her to try to escape. He wondered if her tribe was among the Indians with Quick Thunder. But he had not tied her. When the fighting started, he'd said, "You can go if you like. We may be all killed. Yes, you can go."

She had said nothing, only looked at him with quick eyes.

Suddenly, Windy Mandalian was at his side, lying down beside him to peer out through the two fallen trees that formed the protection. "How you doin' there, sharp-shooter?"

Otio grinned. "Sharp—?"

"You shoot sharp."

"Yes."

"How's your ammo?"

"Ciriaco is counting."

"I'll be back," Windy said. "I've got something for the lieutenant." And he was gone.

In another minute or two he was at Matt's side. "Taylor got bogged down with some of the ranchers. Quick Thunder and his boys took a sashay through more than just them couple of outfits we heard about. I told him to get over here fast; should be along directly. Thing is, how do you want him to come in?"

Matt had been studying the fight through his field glasses. "They're working around real carefully to outflank us," he said, still looking through the glasses. Then, putting them down, he said, "Is Taylor coming through the timber? Will he be approaching that way?"

"Why, you want him somewheres else?"

"I want you to get back to him fast and tell him to hold, just back of the timber."

"What about them hostiles?" Windy nodded toward the area Matt had been studying. "They get us outflanked, we'll be out of business real fast."

"We'll just let them."

"I see you got men working across that other side there. You figuring to outflank Quick Thunder while he thinks he's got you pinched?"

"That's about it. We'll let the Sioux think they've got us outflanked. But get Taylor up there fast and have him hold. And then when we bugle it, he can come right in on them."

Windy spat. He spat quickly, for he was in a hurry to say something. "By God, you're getting to be almost as smart as old Windy, by God!"

Billy had collected all the guns of the Cohoes cowboys while Elihu Cohoes and Ching Domino glared in fury. But twice Larrabee Hogan had to tell his brother to move faster. When finally the weapons had been placed in the chuckwagon, Hogan stepped in closer toward the men, while at a signal from him, the other Cohoes drovers, who had been left with the herd, came in.

"Here is the way it is going to be." Larrabee Hogan made a movement with the Winchester. "Come in a little closer there. Now I've already told these here men that we're going to push the herd up to the Stinking Water, and when it is sold you'll all be paid what Cohoes promised you — plus a bonus for good behavior." His grin was wicked. "And for bad behavior, you'll get this." He patted the barrel of the .44-40. The grin widened. "In the guts, so you'll remember it." He glanced over at his young brother. "You growed pretty good, Billy boy."

Billy stood looking at his brother. Yes, the same Larry. Smiling, laughing, joking, tough, cruel, unforgiving — all of it still there. But Billy wished he hadn't gathered up those guns.

"Get the team hitched to the chuckwagon, kid, and you'll drive. I want someone I can trust holding those weapons."

Billy started toward the chuckwagon. He was almost there when he stopped and turned to face his brother.

"Larry, I got to get back to my outfit."

"This *is* your outfit."

"Larry, I'm talking about my platoon. The army."

"Bullshit, kid. Get them horses hitched up."

Billy felt something strong moving in his chest, in his belly and legs. "I'm in the army, Larry. I'm a soldier. I have got my duty to 'tend to."

"Billy, I am telling you just once again — get them horses hitched. We are moving out. I mean fast."

Kincaid, watching the Sioux through the glasses, began to wonder if he hadn't made the wrong decision. There was the sign from Windy that Taylor and the Second had reached the far side of the timber, and meanwhile the hostiles had almost completely outflanked his position. His own men, moving out on the right, had nearly completed a wider flank on the Sioux. Now the firing had become sporadic, as the sun began to dip down the sky.

And suddenly there was Windy, signaling from the

edge of the timber that Taylor was in position. Matt watched the warriors still moving on his two flanks now, with his own men farther out on the right.

"Corporal McBride, blow the bugle like you never blew it before!"

"Yessir!"

As the notes of the bugle cut into the afternoon sky, Taylor and his men came charging out of the timber to the complete surprise of the Sioux, who had been so sure of a complete wipeout of the soldiers. At the same time, the men on the right, widely outflanking the enemy, now poured rifle fire into the startled Sioux from their rear.

At the timber edge, Windy dropped down beside Otio. "Challenge you to a shootin' party," he declared.

The Basque's wide face split into a grin. "I shoot one, then you shoot one."

"I'll take that tall bugger over there on the brown and white pony," Windy said, raising his Sharps. And he blew the warrior right off his horse.

"I take that one there." And Otio shot a running warrior who was trying to get in close.

It didn't last long. The fight was brisk and furious, and then a shout went up from the men of Easy Company when, without warning, Quick Thunder and his warriors raced away. The fight was over.

Taylor, coming up to Matt, could barely raise his wounded arm, which, although on the mend, had stiffened. Taylor managed his salute finally. He was glad that Kincaid said nothing. He would have been disappointed to find a weakness in his superior officer.

Billy had not hitched the team to the wagon. He had suddenly started walking toward his brother.

"Kid..."

"Larry, if I go with you, it makes me a deserter."

"Don't worry about it. We're going to have that spread we always talked about. Remember?"

He was close to his brother now, and looking into Larry's eyes, he felt a sudden chill running all through him. Larrabee Hogan's eyes were brilliant, wild, and very wide. For an instant, Billy was terrified, but then he felt something take hold of him, and he was absolutely calm as he spoke.

"Larry, it's too late. You're no longer nineteen. You're what you are, and the law will come for you. The soldiers will come. The firing up there has stopped." And Billy felt something break and start to melt in him. He stared at his brother, the brother who had raised him; and he didn't know what to do or say. All he could do now was try not to cry.

His brother's grin was wild, like it had been cut into his face. "You gonna arrest me, soldier?"

Billy shook his head. "I just want you to let me go. And you better ride out of here fast."

"Sorry, kid. I've waited one hell of a long time for this."

Billy wanted to say something, but he didn't trust himself not to break down. He turned, hoping his legs would support him as he started toward his horse, his back toward his brother.

"Billy!"

But the shot that rang out was not from Larrabee Hogan's gun. Billy, realizing he was still alive, turned, his eyes jumping with disbelief as he saw Larry falling to his knees, blood flowing out of his mouth, his hands clawing toward his neck.

"Hold it, kid!"

It was Elihu Cohoes who, standing by the chuckwagon, was covering him with a .45.

"Jesus!" Ching Domino stood rooted where he was.

"They was too interested in their conversation," Cohoes said. "Family does that to you, you know. Now we can just go back to where we was."

Ching Domino started to move toward the chuckwagon.

"Where you going?"

"To pick up my hardware." Domino was still staring at Cohoes and the .45. Billy had knelt down beside his dead brother.

"You can first take that hardware off the soldier boy there," Cohoes said.

Ching Domino couldn't believe what he had seen. Cohoes! Why, Cohoes handled that weapon like it was a part of him! But he turned his attention now to the young soldier kneeling beside Hogan. Billy got slowly to his feet.

"I'll take that gun," Ching Domino said. "Just unbuckle your belt and let 'er fall."

For a moment Billy just looked at the approaching gunfighter, with Cohoes covering him from behind. He was remembering what Larry had taught him: always stay loose, use whatever cover was handy, and try to get the other fellow off balance.

"Mister," Billy Golightly said, "you can go piss up a rope. You are not taking any gun off the United States Army."

"Do as he says, soldier boy!"

And then Billy Golightly said something that startled him even as the words came out. "Cohoes and Domino—you are both under arrest."

The surprise on Ching Domino's face turned into a big grin as he closed in on Billy, and just for an instant he was in direct line with Cohoes. In that flashing moment, Billy Golightly, loose as a rope, drew, stepping to his right, and drilled Elihu Cohoes right in his gunhand. And

175

in the same movement, without even a breath between, he smashed Ching Domino in the belly with the Scoff, and as the big man grunted, bending a little, he raked the gun barrel across his jaw.

Billy Golightly was well in charge of the situation when Matt Kincaid, Windy Mandalian, and the men of his own platoon rode in.

twenty-one

Captain Warner Conway, easing forward in his swivel chair, drew thoughtfully and with great pleasure on his first cigar of the day. Releasing a plume of smoke, he leaned his elbow on the desk before him and regarded the ash to see if the fine Havana was burning evenly.

"Well now, if we can believe Private Golightly," he said, looking at Matt and Windy Mandalian, "and I do, then how do we explain Hogan acting in such a crazy way? Didn't he realize what any ten-year-old would understand, that if the army didn't catch up with him and that herd of cattle, the Sioux would. He must have been out of his head."

"Well, sir," said Matt. "I think that's what Golightly must have been getting at when he spoke about the crazy look in his brother's eyes." He glanced over at Windy. "How do you see it, scout?"

"Dunno. I only know what I hear. Never knew Golightly, and of course none of us knowed Hogan. But he sounds kind of like a good man gone wrong. Happens." He paused and rubbed the end of his nose with the back of his hand. "Excepting I've a notion Larrabee Hogan maybe didn't go so wrong as it might appear."

"How do you mean that?"

"Well, like I say, I don't know Golightly, but what he done, he stuck with the army. He showed his guts. I think you can say that."

"I'm with that," said Conway, and Matt nodded.

"And he said his brother raised him."

"From a button, as he put it," said Conway with a faint smile.

Windy reached for his chewing tobacco, and Conway sighed. "Please finish what you started to say, Windy. I mean," he went on quickly, "you've got us hanging on a cliff."

"I just said it." And Windy squinted at his skinning knife, testing the blade with his callused thumb. "And my question to you gentlemen is, do you think Larrabee Hogan did a fair to good job on his kid brother?"

Matt Kincaid grinned all over his face at the scout's words, and Warner Conway chuckled.

"He is a kid, you know," the captain said. "I had Ben Cohen check again with regiment."

"He is under age, then?" Matt asked.

Captain Conway nodded. "He is under age, and you, Lieutenant Kincaid, and myself"—and he smiled broadly—"are over."

The three of them laughed at the captain's reference to himself and Matt being over age in grade.

"This, of course," continued Conway, "is between the two of us and our scout here, not to mention Ben Cohen."

"Regiment knows nothing, then," said Matt. "Is that what you're saying, sir?"

"Let me put it this way—they revealed young Golightly's age to our first sergeant without realizing that they were doing so."

This brought another appreciative round of laughter from the three of them.

"Our first sergeant is a man of resource, not to say strength and perseverance." And Conway rose and walked to the window that overlooked the parade. Then he turned back to face Windy and Matt. "When you gentlemen have a moment, and if you feel so inclined later in the day, you might take a walk out back of the paddock." He paused regarding their raised eyebrows. "There you will see four individuals, including Private Golightly, digging up a large section of the prairie—with spoons."

Windy wagged his head, and Matt released a sigh.

"As Ben put it," Conway continued, "it would not be fair to any of them—and especially to young Golightly—were he to let them forget and be forgiven the punishment he had meted out prior to the engagement with the Sioux. It will, Sergeant Cohen assured me, set a good example to the men, and especially to the newest recruit, that army discipline prevails, come hell, high water, or Indian attack."

And again the three men broke into laughter at the singlemindedness and hard honesty of Ben Cohen, without whom, they all knew, Easy Company would be infinitely poorer.

"And what about Cohoes and Domino?" Windy asked as the captain started toward the door of his office.

"They'll remain under special surveillance, along with their men and cattle, while Regiment investigates."

"That will take a while," Matt observed. "Cohoes and Domino are going to be plenty riled at missing their sale."

Captain Conway opened the door of his office. He reached up and took the cigar from his mouth, releasing a great cloud of smoke.

"Tough," he said.

Later that same morning the delegate for the Wyoming Territory shook hands warmly with the commanding officer of Easy Company and his adjutant, and then stepped into the waiting ambulance that would take him and his daughter to regimental headquarters.

"I thank you again, Captain Conway," Hawes Thatcher

said, leaning forward so he could have a last word, while the gate of Outpost Number Nine was being opened.

"It was our pleasure, Mr. Thatcher—and Miss Thatcher."

Hawes Thatcher turned briefly to his daughter, seated beside him.

"Thank you so much, Captain Conway and Lieutenant Kincaid," the girl said, giving them each her very best smile. "And you are definitely invited to the wedding."

"And we are definitely accepting," said Warner Conway. "I hope you can arrange what we spoke of, sir."

Thatcher smiled. "No trouble, Captain. We'll just have to break the news to Mrs. Thatcher, Julie's mother, and make arrangements for the ceremony at Fort Laramie."

"And the groom, sir," Matt cut in. "Don't forget the groom."

Hawes Thatcher boomed out a great laugh. "Your end will take care of a furlough, of course; and, uh, I will handle the legal red tape." He chuckled and—neither Matt nor Conway could believe it—dropped a fast wink. "After all, isn't that what a delegate is for, gentlemen?"

As they watched the ambulance go through the gate, Matt said, "Captain, with a father-in-law like that, Private Billy Golightly is going to think Sergeant Ben Cohen's shit detail is a sweetheart."

"I know what you mean," the captain replied as they both turned back toward the orderly room.

"On the other hand," Matt said, "it could be like Windy said. Maybe Larrabee Hogan's kid brother might be just what'll make the mare go."

It was the following morning when Matt Kincaid and Windy Mandalian rode up the rise of ground toward where the stand of timber looked down on the river.

"Looks like they pulled out already," Windy said as they sat their horses.

"Well, he did say they'd be heading back to the Sierras."

"True enough. He didn't say whether they'd be back."

Windy kicked his roan forward, and Matt fell in beside him as they rode up to the top of the rise and through the burnt-out timber. Presently they broke out on the prairie again.

Now, sitting their horses, they looked out across the rolling land. It was a day in which nothing seemed to move, and yet everything was in motion. The wind stirred ever so slightly, riffling the tawny grass. Even the sky seemed to shimmer as they looked across the great stretch of prairie.

"They are really gone," Matt said. He found himself wishing they'd had a chance to say goodbye.

"Maybe," Windy said. "Shit, you know how the prairie is."

They had been there about ten minutes when suddenly they saw something moving. It was the sheep, the mules, and the herders coming up out of a draw, a good distance away, so that they were almost specks. But they were clearly visible.

The party moved up the long lip of the draw and, reaching the top, were clear against the horizon, then presently they started down another draw, slowly moving out of view.

Matt was about to suggest that they follow, but somehow the feeling he got from Windy, and now found in himself, kept him from speaking.

"He was a good man," Windy said.

"Wish I'd gotten to know him," Matt replied.

"You know him." Windy spat. He wiped his mouth with the back of his hand. "Know what?"

"What?"

"I was just wondering what happened to that little Indian gal."

Matt was silent as now they both sat there in their saddles watching the sheep, the mules, the herders disappear over the edge of the distant draw.

"You know what?" Windy spat again.

"What?"

"You know him, same as I know him. So we know what happened to that little girl."

They waited a moment longer, and then they turned their mounts and rode back to Outpost Number Nine.

Watch for

EASY COMPANY
AT HAT CREEK STATION

twenty-second novel in the exciting
EASY COMPANY series from Jove

coming in November!

MORE ROUGH RIDING ACTION FROM JOHN WESLEY HOWARD